£2

Voyage with Jason

Ken Catran is an award-winning television writer, who also enjoys the diversity and challenge of writing young adult fiction. His previous books include *Golden Prince* and *Talking to Blue*.

Ken Catran

Voyage with Jason

Flyways

First published in Australia in 2000
by Thomas C. Lothian Pty Ltd, Port Melbourne
First published in the United Kingdom in 2001
by Flyways, an imprint of Floris Books

British Library CIP Data available

ISBN 0–86315–345–3

Printed in Great Britain
by Bookcraft, Bath

Part One

Pylos is my name. All the name I have. And this story was mine before the bards shaped it into legend; the legend of Jason and Heracles and all the Argonaut heroes who dared the unknown seas for gold and glory ... and who were all touched by the dark cold power of the Gods and by fate.

... There was once a king of Greece who took a second wife. She hated the children of his first wife, who were called Prixus and Helle. She sought their deaths, but the Gods intervened ...

They escaped, on the back of a wonderful, golden-fleeced, winged ram. They flew long long leagues to the unknown ...

On the journey, little Helle lost her handhold and fell. The place where she drowned is now called Hellespont Straits. The winged ram took Prixus on, to a far country called Colchis ...

And what became of that wonderful winged ram? And why did King Pelias of Icolos fear the coming of a man with one sandal ...? The legend and this story are bound up with mine. And with a journey to the unknown lands of a dark, ageless power ...

A voyage with Jason.

Chapter 1

There were giants in those dark undiscovered lands. And creatures with six arms, a sword in each; coasts of black sand and high mountains that spat red fire into the sky. Dark magic places and darker mystery. That was why we were building this ship. To journey to those places ...

Where no ship returned from.

All spring I had worked on this ship, its ribs like a giant wooden fish-skeleton around me. I could dream about going on a journey to unknown lands. But my dreams always ended with a hard thump on my back and a hoarse bellow.

'Dreaming again, little rat!'

The monsters of that unknown land could not look more horrible than Thegus. His thick hair was matted with lumps of the black pitch we smeared on the ship's hull. His face was blotchy, his nose broken and his ears bitten from fights. A knife-cut scarred one cheek, and his eyes were red from all that he drank.

'You are the worst apprentice in all Greece! These are nothing but firewood!'

He grabbed one of the pegs I had been cutting and threw it overboard into the dark waters of Corinth harbour. A seagull swooped, then rose up shrieking, sounding insulted.

The other workers watched, snickering. When Thegus abused me, he left them alone. He was foreman and I hated him. He was always pushing up against me, stinking of sweat and bad beer. Sometimes he even stopped my evening meal of lentils and onions. With his black shadow over me, I forgot my dreams.

'Fifty more pegs cut before sunset,' he snarled. 'Use this wood.'

Wooden ships are held together with wooden pegs. Better than metal and less expensive. But looking at the wood he gave me — fifteen summers and half-trained — even I knew something was wrong. The wood pale, fresh-cut, still oozing sap. No good to hold the ribs of a ship.

If I said this to Thegus, he would just kick me. Anyway, he was a master craftsman and must have known. So I cut and chipped with my bronze hammer and chisel but it was useless. The wood was too green and would shrink when dry. The planks it held would loosen and let in the sea. I kept cutting, gashing my hand once.

At sunset, Thegus banged his hammer on the deck to cease work. The workers left quickly enough and Thegus's black shadow came across me again. I still had twenty pegs to cut but threw down my chisel and turned.

'Foreman Thegus, this wood is no good for pegs,' I said.

Thegus squatted, his hairy legs wide under his leather kilt. He puffed his blotchy cheeks and smirked. I was expecting to be kicked and his answer surprised me.

'Of course not, Pylos.' Even using my name. 'The first storm wave will let in Sea God Poseidon's anger. All will drown.'

'Does Shipwright Argus know this?' I asked.

Argus was a tall thin-faced man with a bitter-twisting mouth. A good shipwright, crawling over our wood-boned fish every day, though he never noticed me. Thegus shrugged, his voice still mild.

'That is not your concern. Finish the pegs and you will have a good meal tonight in my shelter. Salt fish, olives and carrots, even some wine, eh?'

Nothing would get me near his shelter. And I was sick of this. I was Greek, freeborn, even though he treated me like a slave, this sweat-smelling pig of a Thracian. I threw down my chisel.

'I will not make pegs to sink a ship!'

Thegus leaned his face close to me. Close enough for me to see the mixed sweat and oil on his face, the pitch-spots in his thick matted beard. His long bronze dagger creaked a little in its leather scabbard. His eyes were black as charcoal.

'Yes, Pylos. You will.'

His dagger pricked under my chin. I had a moment to nod and say, yes. But my father had drowned; I would not work on a death ship. So I brought my hammer down hard on his toe and ducked under his arm.

It was a mad thing to do. Thegus had bought my apprenticeship from my uncle and was my lawful master. Scrambling across the narrow plank to the jetty, I heard his roar of murderous anger. I still clutched a handful of the pegs, dropping some as I ran.

'I will gut you for this!' he yelled.

I dared a glance back. He was bounding after me, shaggy-bearded and glaring like all the fates.

Glancing back was wrong; I ducked into an alley and hit up against a wagonload of planks bound for Argos. I stopped, stunned, and Thegus grabbed me, his stinking breath close.

'From now on,' he muttered, his dagger pricking again, 'you will be a good boy. Yes?'

I could not nod. Not for this pig and he knew it. His dagger lowered, for a swift belly-cutting slash. In this dark alley, nobody would notice or care. Thegus leered a moment, to draw out the pleasure. Then something hit him in the face.

'What has the boy done to upset you?'

The voice came from the shadows, high-pitched but strong, like shallow ocean waves on a rock. Another 'sputting' sound and something bounced on Thegus's big nose. An olive stone.

Now I could see sandalled feet jutting out of a deep narrow side-door; somebody sitting there, quietly watching us.

Thegus turned, dagger in hand. 'Shut up! Or you'll get the same!'

A loud sigh came from the dark doorway and the sandals scrambled upright. A man shambled out on the stone cobbles and stood there, blinking. He was shorter than Thegus, with frizzy dark hair and black stubble over a square chin; his nose flat as though it had been broken several times; small blue eyes that always blinked. His voice was mild.

'The same what?' Dressed in a smelly hide tunic; a shepherd from the hills with his flocks for market. A simple stupid man who knew nothing of city evil. 'If the boy has done harm, he must go before the judges.'

A simple village solution. The man held a long

knotted ashwood shaft and laid it aside; stepped forward, taking another olive from his pouch and popping it in his mouth. He blinked, smiled, as though the matter was solved.

Thegus smiled back; the smile of a wolf seeing a lamb. He closed one hand around my throat, choking off speech. I knew what would happen now. The peasant would step closer and Thegus lunge with his dagger. A killing stroke, then he would finish me, because of those pegs. No witnesses. Choked, glassily numb, I watched as the whole thing happened.

Thegus took a step back, smiling. His dagger hand to side. The stranger shambled closer, up came the dagger, quicker than it takes to tell this. Spots of black light danced on my eyes as my breath failed. A hard thump-thump and the pressure on my throat eased. The stone wall slid up my back as I collapsed hard on the stinking cobbles. Stunned, waiting for the killing stroke. Waiting long enough for my vision to clear.

Thegus was slammed against the wall, his dagger on the ground, his wrist broken, his bearded mouth gasping with pain. 'Shepherd' had taken his dagger, broken his wrist and punched him, all at once. Now he bent over, jabbing the dagger into the cobbles, snapping the blade. He stood up and blinked at me.

'Boy, is there a decent food house near here?'

We left Thegus groaning on the cobbles. I took him to a snack bar, run by a sailor whose foot was cut off in a fight with pirates. He called his horsemeat beef, but it was better than most. His place was low-ceilinged, lit with guttering lamps whose mutton fat stink filled the air. Tonight, it was packed with Sidon sailors, gurgling the thick barley beer. They scowled because Sidon sailors do not like sharing anything, even the places they drink.

My shepherd friend had not even told me his name. He blinked in the low light and shouldered to a table. The owner came over, very fat, with sweat and grease oozing from every fold of flesh.

'Food,' said Shepherd.

The owner stood there until Shepherd rang a copper piece on the table. The open chink of his pouch revealed more pieces. The noise drew the attention of the Sidon sailors.

'Where did you get those?' I whispered.

A simple sheep-herder would not have metal to trade. Shepherd just blinked sleepily and our meal came. A wooden bowl of mutton — not very much mutton — with onions, cabbage and garlic, swimming in fat. A round hard pancake of bread.

'I can't pay for this,' I whispered.

'I'll eat what you leave,' he replied.

I was beginning to understand his simple-mad humour. So I spooned up some of the stew and chewed on the flat bread. Shepherd ate his with much lip-smacking, then stretched his legs in the filthy straw and shouted for wine.

The Sidon sailors were still watching. I knew what would happen. Soon, they would pick a fight and rob him of his money. Share it with the owner — for his silence. I whispered this to Shepherd but he just smacked his lips louder, as though he could fight all six. He shouted again and those shaven-heads made their move.

They came over. All stocky and tough, each one a match even for Thegus. Shepherd had his face in the wine-bowl, the sticky liquid over his stubbled chin. As he tipped it into his mouth, his sleeve fell back from his thick muscular arm, showing the blue outline of a tattoo.

They stopped.

I did not see the tattoo properly. Shepherd lowered the wine cup, blinking at them. And those tough seamen shuffled like naughty children. 'Melkarth,' one whispered and slowly, awkwardly, they remembered their unfinished drinks at the end of the bar.

'Melkarth? Is that your name?' I asked.

Shepherd guzzled the last wine. 'Give me that peg,' he said.

All this was a strange mad dream. I had no home tonight, no work; Thegus still out there somewhere. So, caught in the strange dream, I passed the peg over. He squeezed it between his fingers and nodded, blinking.

'That man chased you because of the bad pegs?' I nodded and he blinked again. 'Prince Jason should know about this.'

Jason! Captain of our near-completed ship, leader to the unknown lands! I gasped and choked. I did not want to see him. Princes and kings led a life apart, living by different rules. Even half-mad Shepherd should know this. I swallowed the last piece of bread, thinking hard.

Jason was up in the palace on the hill. So I could sit here a little time, my stomach full. Sneak away, find a ship, or walk the roads to another city.

Shepherd yawned and got up. The Sidon sailors moved uneasily, again that muttered 'Melkarth.' I got up too, looking at the door. Time to run. I moved quick.

Shepherd moved quicker. He grabbed and slung me over his shoulder, like a workman with his tool-bag. He walked out, ducking his head under the low doorway. I banged mine but he did not care. He set off up the hill, me carried light as a bag of onions. My head somewhere down his back, I smelled the stink of his lion-hide tunic.

'I don't want to go to the palace,' I yelled.

'I do,' as though that settled the matter.

'They will beat you!' I shouted.

'Perhaps, boy.' Obviously he had drunk more wine than was good for him.

I yelled that the palace was different to the town. There, our King Pelias decided life or death. He had too many warriors, even for Shepherd. They had leather-bronze armour and long spears that would sink into our bodies.

'I don't want to die!' I yelled.

'Neither do I,' he replied.

Despite my weight, he broke into a trot up the slope. A madman, but I made one last appeal to his sanity. 'They will kill you!' That did not work. 'Melkarth, sailors may be scared of you, but not kings!'

The road steepened but he kept trotting, with the strength of a bear. Dark shadows of night, the pale moon overhead. Kings always make the road to their stronghold difficult. Now the heavy-blocked masonry walls loomed, the gate before us, set with a carved stone ram. The gates still stood open because guests were arriving for a banquet.

'They will kill us both!'

'Perhaps.'

He threw me down at the gate, the guards surrounding us in their high horsehair-crested helmets. Their long bronze spearpoints flashed in the torchlight. Their faces were grim and cold as death.

'I want to speak to King Pelias,' said Shepherd.

'Yes?' A guardsman, his eyes careful, his spear rock-steady. 'Go away. Think yourselves lucky we have eaten our dinners and are in a good mood.'

'King Pelias,' repeated Shepherd.

'Your business?' growled the guardsman.

'This.' Shepherd held up the peg. 'A gift for the king.'

The onlookers tittered. The guardsman frowned and jabbed. Just hard enough to prick Shepherd. Instead, the spearhead snapped. Shepherd had grabbed it; broke the elm-wood shaft easily as snapping a dry twig. The guardsman went cross-eyed a moment and his growl became uncertain.

'What name do I give King Pelias?'

He took a step backwards as he said this. As though he already knew the answer. All the bronze spearpoints around us lowering.

Shepherd gave his name. Not 'Melkarth' as the Phoenicians knew him, but a name known all over Greece; one that made the spearpoints drop further; uttered so easily that all his antics made sense.

'Heracles.'

Chapter 2

Heracles! I had no time to look up, even to think. Ebony doors inlaid with spirals of bronze gilt swung open. Heracles carried me across flat paving stones polished to a blue sheen. Another set of doors, these inlaid with silver, opened into the feasting hall. Heracles' grip was gentle, but strong as a bronze chain. Together we went into a blare of noise, music, voices, a sudden warmth hitting me. Over it all, loud as thunder, Heracles yelled.

'Jason!'

After the thunder clap there is always stillness. A moment for me to glance around. Peasant boys do not often glimpse the inside of a royal palace. It was big and circular, blazing everywhere with colour. The floor spread out in wavy dot patterns of red, black and blue around a huge circular hearth burning more charcoal than my village would in a year. The smells were rich too, oil and roast food and perfumes.

The walls of this shining magical place danced with black rearing horses and tan antelopes, circling white eagles, and black dolphins in blue-washed water. Proud warrior images that seemed to glare sidelong at me. As Heracles carried me forward, I ducked a look at the people on the raised dais, over the fire.

In the centre throne was King Pelias. Tall, big-nosed, his curly black hair braided with gold wire. He was looking at Heracles, his wide mouth curved with frowning thought. In his hand he held a wine cup that flashed like golden fire in the torchlight. Torches blazed everywhere. Beside him sat his queen, who I had not seen before.

Her wide eyes and black-etched eyebrows gave her painted face a surprised look. Her eyes were green as a moody sea, her mouth painted red. She wore a tight low dress clasped close at the waist, her bare breasts powdered with gold. Gold! Gold rings on her fingers, gold jewellery on her arms, around her neck, in her ears; worth more than a hundred villages. Her staring eyes flashed at me and I lowered my eyes. A voice spoke, ending the silence.

'Heracles. You are always welcome.' It was a young voice, deep and strong, amused like the chuckle-sound of creekwater. 'Sit beside me and eat.' I had heard that voice before, on the ship, talking to Argus. Jason.

He sprawled in his seat, gangly and loose, never showing the grace princes should have. His white linen tunic was stitched with a pattern of black horses, his long dark hair hung down to his shoulders and he wore no gold. But around his neck was a brown leather sandal on a flax string — the strangest ornament I had ever seen. Now he looked at me, with brown-black eyes.

'Who is this, Heracles? Another of your labours?'

A shout of laughter broke the stillness. The King of Tiryns had given Heracles special tasks to perform. Catch a sacred deer, kill a great lion, even clean out some huge stables. He had done those last two, from the way his lion-hide tunic smelled. Heracles let me slide down to stand beside him. His high-pitched voice was still mild.

'This boy is your best craftsman.'

Now, among the guests, I glimpsed Argus who, from his glare, did recognise me. Heracles made a wooden peg appear in his hand like magic. He held it up in the close oil-smelling silence, then crushed it easily, between forefinger and thumb. Even for the mighty Heracles, it should not have been that easy.

'So. A bad ship peg?' Pelias spoke for the first time, not looking at me. 'Make a seat for Heracles.'

A guardsman reached for me but Heracles blinked at him. He flinched and drew back smartly. Heracles flicked the peg into the charcoal hearth and spoke just above the soft pop it made. 'But a whole bag of these? All ordered by your foreman? What do you make of that, Pelias?'

He did not even give Pelias his title of king. But that was all I heard. I had been inside this strange rich place too long — like a fish on a hook of gold, doomed to die. My knees suddenly weak as seaweed, the red hearth and painted walls spun around. The wavy-patterned floor-tiles came up to hit me, hard as the smack of Heracles' own hand.

Pylos is the name of a Greek state. A good place to live if you are rich or have a skill. If you are a boy whose mother is dead and whose father lost in his fishing boat, then you are just another mouth for your uncle to feed. A better bargain for him to sell you. Thegus called me 'Pylos' because he did not care about my real name.

There was blackness after the palace floor smacked me so hard. Bad dreams, panic like a trapped bird fluttering. Through them a voice asking questions, another voice muttering. Only when I jammed my tongue against my teeth did the second voice stop. It was me doing the muttering. I opened my eyes.

Morning. I was in the outer part of the palace where the sleep places are, wrapped in a good woollen blanket. And squatting before me was Jason. He rocked on his heels, dressed in a plain workday leather tunic and pointed cap, the leather sandal no longer around his neck; in his hand, another of those greenwood pegs.

'What were you going to do with this, Pylos?' he asked.

A wonderful chance to say I was looking for him. But his eyes were dark as our great sea when a storm is coming. This was not a man to lie to.

'Nothing. I was scared and my stomach was empty.'

'Honest words, Jason,' came an amused voice. 'You will not hear many of those in a palace.'

An olive stone landed on my knee. Heracles was sprawled near me, still clad in his smelly hide. He flicked another olive into his mouth, chewed and spat the stone against a marble pillar.

'Pylos, do not mind this fool,' said Jason easily. 'The Gods have addled his wits like sour milk. You knew these pegs would sink *Argos* and were coming to tell me. Yes?'

'I would never have dared come near the palace,' I muttered.

Jason was testing me but I did not realize it. He always had to know about people. He grinned, his big white teeth showing. 'Maybe you would have,' he said. 'Maybe.'

Heracles spat out another stone. 'Ask Thegus why he ordered the pegs made.'

'I would,' said Jason. 'But Thegus is gone.'

A week later the deck-planks of *Argos* were laid, the hull tarred black and huge eyes painted on the bows. Ships must be able to see where they are going. Heracles pulled me everywhere — even fed me, like a master with his dog — in his casual way, protecting me. It was rumoured King Pelias ordered the bad pegs so that Jason's voyage would fail. That was when I learned about the sandal Jason always wore.

First I learned about the crew Jason gathered, a special band of heroes to face those unknown dangers. Masters of the sword and spear, whose names were already household words. Castor and Pollux, twin princes from Sparta, great boxers. Zetes and Calais, fleetest of runners. Telamon, master bowman. Orpheus, a round-faced bard, whose lute could charm fish from water. All were highborn and famous.

How wonderful to be in their company! Perhaps one day all Greece would talk about me! Heracles thought differently about a hero crew.

'Put a lion in a leather bag with a wolf,' he said. 'Add a ram, a shark and a bull. Shake the bag well and you have the crew of *Argos*.' His shout of laughter sounded across the blue Icolos bay.

In the bay, Jason had hired a galley and was teaching his princes and heroes to row together. They were more used to shouting their own commands than rubbing their backsides raw like this.

They cursed and squabbled, elbowed each other on the benches. The oar-beat splashed like a drunken crab and Heracles laughed again.

'Ask me why they put up with that,' he said, flicking me an olive.

I put it in my mouth. 'Why?'

Heracles rolled his eyes, spat an olive stone high and caught it. 'Because south of here, many days' sail, is a pair of straits. Pinched narrow as rabbit guts and ruled by a powerful city, Troy. Slip between those straits and there is a new great sea. Magic lands of gold. Every city king wants to know about it. So all send a prince or noble.' He flicked the stone high in the air. 'But first they must learn to pull together.'

His laughter sounded over the clear blue water, over the curses and mis-timed splashes of that noble crew.

Two black bulls were sacrificed at the launch. Their red blood spurted on the slipway and *Argos* slid down, splashing full-breasted into the water. It groaned, and the townsfolk shuddered. But all ships make this birth noise when they are set on the water.

King Pelias was there, in black armour and a gold ram's head helmet that masked his eyes. He flashed like a demon and I kept in Heracles' massive shadow. Orpheus shook his hair from his face and drew his fingers lightly over the lute strings.

Until then, *Argos* was not a ship. Our heroes and princes still fought over their rowing places. But as the black-tarred keel settled in the water, something magic happened. Orpheus's lute song rang in silver clear notes that splashed to different sounds; like a mast being stepped, of taut new ropes and a flapping full sail. All the oars splashed together as *Argos* drew into the bay. Loud cheering from the townsfolk but Pelias was silent behind his gold mask.

My dreams of being among them were fading. Heracles had a rowing partner too, a young man with black ringlets, named Hylas. He had clever comic features and was a real squire who knew how to look after the arms and armour of his lord. Old enough to be a good companion. Heracles drew in men like a sun sucking shadow. So I thought about leaving.

It was easy enough. The night before sailing, I stayed on board and filled a bag from the stores. I would be leagues down the road by morning. But a shadow came over and a hand touched my shoulder. It was Jason and he knew what I was doing. He sat beside me and touched the sandal on its thong.

'Pylos, do you know why I wear this?'

Heracles had told me. Jason was brought up in distant Thessaly but was the true heir to Icolos. King Pelias had stolen his birthright and he was back to claim it. But, wading a river, he lost a sandal, and Pelias — who was very superstitious — had heard a prophecy that a one-sandalled man would cause his doom. So their fates were linked and Jason wore the sandal to remind Pelias of this.

'Why doesn't he take a chance and kill you?' I asked. It was a natural question.

Jason laughed. 'Kings think more deeply than that. I am a Master Seaman so Pelias sends me to the unknown sea. If I come back with a cargo of gold — that will be the time to kill me.' He grinned. 'Since you spoiled his little accident. Now take the food if you want to.'

I sat there, feeling miserable and alone. I think Jason sensed this and he nudged me lightly. 'You ran with those pegs like a boy. You kept to Heracles like a boy. Come on this voyage and you'll return a man. That's the best reward I can give you.' He pressed a gold seal into my hand. 'Or take the road.'

He was gone, quickly and quietly. I sat there, thinking. Heracles had cared for me like a stray puppy. Jason was giving me the chance to be some-body. No longer a 'boy.' But on a voyage that might take all our lives. Thinking about this, I fell asleep. I woke to the creak and snap of a live ship, gliding on blue water in the blue-dark dawn.

We had slipped away quietly in case Pelias changed his mind. A good sea wind was taking us along the headland, the crew bundled in their cloaks. Hylas and Heracles were laughing quietly at some private joke. The others ignored me, except for a little brown-faced man whose name was Butes — an expert beekeeper, of all things — and he winked at me. Then Jason called from the stern.

'Hey, Pylos! Are we putting you ashore, then?'

I stood up, still feeling alone. All the heroes ignored me, beneath their notice. I walked down to the stern, trying not to trip as Hylas stuck his leg out. Jason was with Steersman Tiphys, a thick-shouldered red-faced giant with thinning fair hair.

'I want to go with you.'

I held out his gold seal but he pushed my hand back

and grinned. He knew I would stay. He grinned, looking over at the headland and his grin went. He pointed.

'Look, Pylos. An old friend is saying goodbye.'

We were rounding the headland and a last unpleasant surprise waited: Thegus, jeering and dancing up and down, his right forearm splinted. We would never return, he jeered, yelling horrible insults, raising his leather kilt and turning to show his backside. He felt safe doing this at such a distance but forgot *Argos* was a crew of masters. A twang as Telamon, master archer, strung his bow and took up an arrow.

'Loose your shaft on the upward roll of the ship,' shouted Tiphys, the steering oars gripped tight.

'You mind the ship, I will mind the shooting,' snapped Telamon. The answer of one master to another.

He balanced only a moment then drew and loosed. His arrow flew up, against the wind. Too much distance to carry, I thought. Wrong! Thegus had just showed his dirty backside again and the arrow swooped down. His howl of pain came back on the wind and we laughed and clapped. Telamon unstrung his bow with a grim smile. A master shot!

The howls faded behind us as the headland slipped away. Men laughed, full of pleasure because a good adventure lay ahead. Soon enough the happiness would go. But right now we could all laugh as our splendid ship cut the green-black water. The painted yellow eyes glared over the waves. A good voyage, I thought, to take me to manhood.

And it would. But the way was marked with blood.

Chapter 3

Those first voyage days were good. *Argos* was a big ship, half a length longer than any I had seen. But its broad-stroked oar power must thrust against strong currents when we reached that strait. It was far ahead, though, and even I knew these coasts. No monsters, only the happy bottle-nosed dolphins leaping ahead of the prow.

The winds were good and there was little rowing. The heroes relaxed, drank wine and took each other's measure. Some brawling too but nobody picked a fight with Pollux, Master Wrestler; and not even Pollux dared challenge Heracles.

Jason stayed aloof. His kingdom was the small stern deck and steering oars. Mostly the heroes kept to their benches because there is little room to move on a galley. My place was everywhere a job needed doing. Greasing the ropes, scrubbing the planks, making fires at the coves we put into each night and cooking the meals. Hard and constant work but better than chipping pegs for Thegus.

And so, from the coast into open sea. Two full days and even the heroes fell silent as the shore dropped away. Open sea is dark and powerful, where Sea God Poseidon dwells. One twitch of his finger would raise up a killing storm.

We slept at sea and there is nowhere comfortable to sleep on a galley. The hard planks and salt spray raised new sores and Butes rubbed mutton fat into mine. He at least noticed me enough for that. To the others, even Heracles, I was still nothing. The boy. Finally, Cape Poseidon loomed ahead in the drifting sea murk.

'Worse than this ahead!' shouted Tiphys merrily.

There was. We were following the old trade route first, to another peninsula. Then four long days of open sea to the island of Lemnos. The wind blew against us and we rowed. The heroes grunted and strained, oars slapping water; their sweat ran like rain streaming from a leather hide.

Only Heracles showed no exhaustion. He was still laughing on the fourth day and I learned something else about him. He used his strength to bully men, to show their own weakness. And they resented him for it.

I found out more about Jason too. About what a captain does. He was always at the steering oar. Looking at the sky, testing the rigging, the sail; the colour of water beneath our keel, even whatever fish showed. He made jokes, praised his crew, knew every man by name. I don't know when he slept.

And the Gods played with us. Let us think the voyage was going well because we were still in known waters. But they were ready with a foretaste of those horrors. It came with the solid dark shape of Lemnos Island before us. A fine big island, famed for its food and wine. So the crew joyfully bent their backs and chanted an oar-stroke song. One two three — stroke! One two three — stroke!

Lemnos would be a good place to stop and rest.

Or so we thought.

I was a peasant boy from a fishing village. So I saw things that warriors did not. And I was first to notice that things were wrong at Lemnos.

The town was set on a good harbour. High walls kept out pirate raiders from the Anatolian mainland. But even the pirates do not go inland. Because Lemnos is also a sacred woman place, with many groves and shrines, guarded by priestesses of the old Mother Goddess. Jason warned us of this as we glided into port. Heracles snorted noisily but the others stayed quiet. Everyone respects the power of Mother Goddess even though All-Father Zeus rules in the sky.

Closer, the town still sleeping in the dawn. No movement, no sign of life. Then I saw a fishing boat by the jetty. The mast not unstepped but leaning over, the rigging rotten. No fisherman leaves his boat like that. Other boats, also derelict, splattered with bird droppings. I whispered this to Jason and he nodded, frowning. He was listening to a strange noise.

To no noise at all. And that was very strange.

All towns wake at dawn. They clatter and bustle with noise because daylight means work. And if sentries see a ship like ours, they cry a warning. Drums are beaten and the guard musters. But there was no sound and nothing stirred till our bow touched the jetty. Then a line of helmeted heads appeared on the battlements. But still without the clatter of weapons or a single drumbeat.

Around me, the warriors took up shield and spear. Jason, armed only with a sword, jumped lightly onto the jetty and they followed. So did I, my ship knife stuck in my belt. On the jetty, they formed into a fighting clump like a bronze spear, with Jason at the point. He looked up to the walls, to the silent heads looking back.

'If we are not welcome, we will go!' he shouted.

Silence. The town gates were before us, inset from the wall and studded with bronze. Too strong for us to batter down. We walked up slowly and I saw the fishing boats more closely. Nobody had been near them for months. A smell of rotting wood, of decay. Then suddenly, though the heads did not move, at last came noise.

A loud squeal, high-pitched as any seabird. The clank-clank of a bronze bolt being withdrawn. Crossbars thumping as they were swung back. A louder squeal from the bronze hinges and the massive gates began to open.

Around me, spears were lowered and shields locked. The harsh exciting sweat-smell of warriors ready for action was in my nose. But no attackers came out as the gates opened. No arrows flew. The gates just opened, beckoning us into the silent streets. And up on the walls, the helmeted heads disappeared.

'Something is wrong,' muttered Castor and his twin growled agreement.

We all knew there was something wrong. Cities do not open their gates like this. But our crew were warriors and princes who did not scare easily. Jason waved his sword, our sandals tramped and our armour clanked as we marched under the stone portal into the city.

I marched behind Jason, my leather cap jammed

over my eyes. Heracles had no shield or spear and clumped his thick ashwood staff beside me. Fierce rousing mutters came from the men — warriors work their temper for battle like stoking a fire. Every man set his face in a ferocious fighting scowl. Their mutters grew more fierce and the warrior-smell stronger.

A wide paved street stretched ahead. It was set with a centre drain and led to a central square. I glanced up but there were no warriors on the walls now. Houses on either side, neatly plastered white and most with a second storey; no faces at the window, no people on their flat roofs.

Perhaps this was a trap but that was puzzling too. Lemnos was a trading island and killing visitors is bad for trade. So we marched on, our tramping feet filling the street with noise. And still no other sound came.

And being peasant-born, I noticed something else that princes would ignore. On each door, by a peg in the centre, hung a little club-shaped object of stone. A hand-grinder. Every peasant hut has one for grinding corn and barley into porridge and flour. My aunt had one and hit my uncle with it, the day he sold me. But she did not keep it on the door. Perhaps in Lemnos, the custom was different.

I would soon find out how different.

'Steady ...' said Jason quietly.

Ahead, the silence was becoming noise. The clank of weapons and shuffling footsteps as a line of warriors filed into the square from narrow side alleys. Our own men tensed. Ahead, the warrior line waited. Ready for us but not shouting war cries like men preparing to fight. Respecting this we slowed and, from their bronze ranks, an armoured figure stepped out. A voice called.

'Jason! News of your voyage came before you! We of Lemnos give you welcome!'

Jason gaped. For the first time I saw him at a loss for words. The warriors before us were in ill-fitting armour not made for them, their breastplates and leg armour tied on with flax cord; the helmets loose or untidily tilted, some over long hair. And the faces above the shield rims were smooth and beardless. It was not a man's voice that spoke to us and there were no men in this battle line.

'Women …' breathed Hylas beside me.

Jason motioned and the *Argos* crew, still tense, raised their spears. There was movement above us, shadows flickering in the morning sun.

The flat rooftops had grown archers and slingers. More women, not in armour, their long skirts tucked into their belts. They lined the houses on both sides and our men growled like winter bears waking up. But the slings were loose, the arrows not on bowstrings. The woman who had spoken came forward.

'I am Queen Hisyphyle. You are our guests.'

Jason stood stock-still a moment. Then I had to skip back as he slung his shield behind him. He took off his helmet, shoving it in my hands, shaking out his long brown hair. Queen Hisyphyle took off her own helmet, shaking out her blonde hair. They smiled at each other.

'A gracious welcome, Queen,' said Jason. 'We are honoured.'

Words never failed him for long. Now there was a shifting and easing of tension, the archers and slingers left the rooftops, all the women taking off their helmets. Heracles still growled a little but it did look like we were welcome on Lemnos.

They had a good feast for us that night. Lamb and pork-meat on skewers and grilled over the charcoal hearth. Sauces of strong herbs I had never tasted before. Lentils, celery, olives, apples stuffed with honey, figs and almonds; more and different food in one night than all my life. And strange just to eat and eat until my belly was full, then eat more. All our noble crew took it for granted.

I was not among them, of course, but in the outer part of the palace, where our weapons were stored because nobody went armed to a feast. Even so, the rich hot smells and warmth flooded out. Castor and Pollux were with me. They said their stomachs were poor and they did not wish to shame their hosts by eating too little. Of course they were there to guard our weapons and ate everything brought to them. The women knew this; just as they knew there was a strong guard on *Argos*.

And still there was no sign of Lemnos men. But Jason had said ask no questions; let the women tell us in their own time. He sat in the place of honour beside Queen Hisyphyle. Now she was splendidly dressed in a robe of purple and gold thread, her yellow hair bound with a headdress of gold wheat sheaves. Between the sheaves, a little shaped object looked familiar.

In the foyer, the women kept piling our plates. A

plump young black-haired one, who I had last seen wielding a sling, gave me another skewer of goat meat. She bent over so that her hair brushed me and I could smell her oil-scented body. Castor nudged me, with a loud whisper, as she left.

'You're in there, boy — if you know how.'

I replied indignantly that I did know, and they both roared with laughter. Castor nearly choked and his brother thumped him on the shoulders. Orpheus came out, unsteady with too much wine, and began tuning his lute.

'Heracles still not happy,' he hiccupped, staggering back inside.

No males at all, even old men or young boys. So when the feast noise died down and the Spartan twins nodded asleep, I crept back up to the inner doorway. The silver notes of Orpheus's lute died away. Queen Hisyphyle began speaking, her voice as sweet as figs and rich as honey.

'Lemnos is a Mother island. The women are proud, so when our men partnered with slave women and threatened our birthright with bastard offspring we took their armour and weapons. At spear-point we drove them to the galleys, their slaves with them — all the men, old and young; we made a clean sweep. We closed the gates of our city against them. Forever.'

Behind me, Castor and Pollux snored gently. I pressed close to the entrance although, now, the rich spicy food smell was making me sick. The Queen's voice, still sweet as golden honey, was saying that the men sailed somewhere distant to hide their shame. And they would never return.

Jason was asking questions now. I heard a tiny clattering and went back to the foyer; saw Castor and Pollux still asleep and the young black-haired woman there with two others. I could have sworn her hand dropped from our weapons but she smiled and clattered our plates loudly. Castor and Pollux grunted awake.

'Are your stomachs full?' she asked.

We nodded and she smiled again, gathering up more plates. As she bent over, a little pendant fell outside her brown linen tunic. Strange-shaped but familiar. And suddenly I was not sure of her smile. It was like the first sense of a sharp squall on the calm blue sea. The women skipped out, all smiling.

I told Castor and Pollux about the men of Lemnos and they had a good laugh. Spartan men, they said, would never let women near their weapons.

From the hall came laughter too, as Jason and the heroes joked. Orpheus sang a little song about how unwise it is for a cheating husband to leave weapons near a proud wife; how the sharp traders of Lemnos got the short end of the bargain. The women loved it, beating time with their wine cups.

Castor and Pollux thumped time and laughed but I still felt uneasy — all the more because I did not know why.

And you will not believe what happened the next day.

That morning, *Argos* no longer rocked at anchor. Jason had her drawn up on the beach and assembled the crew. We would stay a week or so, he said. A pirate fleet from Crete was near and the Lemnos women offered to reprovision our ship, if we stayed till the pirates were gone. A good bargain, he said, and everyone (except Heracles) agreed.

And there would be no lack of willing partners among the women; they made that very clear. So the men spread through the city and the singing and dancing went on all night. Even Hylas was off getting drunk and I slept on *Argos*, with only Heracles for company. He still growled and muttered unhappily but would not say why. The threat of Cretan raiders seemed quickly forgotten, too.

And as I fell asleep, a sharp thought came. The pendant that black-haired girl wore around her neck; those familiar ornaments between the golden corn-sheaves in the Queen's hair. I realized what they were.

Corn grinders.

Chapter 4

We would only stay a few days, said Jason. But the days became weeks and *Argos* went on props to stop her keel rotting on the sand. The weeks became months and the good sailing weather was going. Nor did any Cretan pirates appear, if they ever existed. Even a peasant boy knew the princes and warriors were having too good a time to think about sailing further.

So we passed the winter at Lemnos and the women looked after us well. Every man of *Argos* — even Polyphemus, who was the oldest — was in demand. Except Heracles, who was still moody. Little clumps of women followed him everywhere and just giggled when he roared at them. Jason and Queen Hisyphyle partnered and as winter ran its course, a little bulge came to her belly. A lot of women had the same bulge.

The black-haired serving maid partnered me. Ixlos was her name. She had offered to show me a sacred pool that you could drink from and learn the language of birds. I had always wanted to know what seagulls screamed at us but only half-believed her.

At the pool, she pushed me in and grabbed my body. I didn't learn the language of birds but did twitter a bit.

After that, I went with Ixlos many times. She was the daughter of a priestess — there were many in Lemnos — and was deep, under her teasing bright manner. We did not see the priestesses often — most times they kept to their secret places. And always Ixlos wore her corn grinder pendant. When I asked her what it meant, she laughed. A symbol of bread-making, the most important work of life.

Heracles still muttered this was not right. But nobody was listening to him now; though a new season of sailing weather was nearly with us, nobody wanted to leave. Orpheus sang that the Gods guided us here. Hisyphyle told us that Troy, a powerful city, barred the unknown straits and knew we were coming. Beyond that were only wild lands and strange creatures. No gold.

Ixlos's father had left the family fishing boat behind and it was a good one. I could marry her and be a man of standing. A better prospect, she said, than leaving my bones on unknown coasts. With no proper grave, my spirit would wander forever.

A lot of the crew wanted to stay now. Even Jason, who would be a king if he took wedding vows with Hisyphyle. So Heracles slept alone on *Argos* and even Hylas laughed at his muttering.

I dreamed of my great good fortune and forgot about corn grinders.

So, one spring morning, I slept late. Ixlos and her mother were gone when I woke. Yes, I thought, the unknown lands could keep their secrets; fishing was a man's life too. So I looked for Ixlos to tell her I would take the vows.

I could not find her anywhere. Sometimes she just vanished and this was one such time. I went out of town, to the pool that was our meeting place. A garland of flowers, plaited in her special way, floated in the water. Perhaps she had knelt here, praying for something. I grinned broadly; today I would be the answer to that prayer.

I went further up the hill. I saw her very high on the ridge a moment, skirts tucked into her belt for ease of walking. I grinned again and began to follow. Perhaps, high up there, we would have another special place. And this time I would surprise her, as she surprised me.

It was a long climb and the upper levels were forest. Still no sign of Ixlos and I went further. Below was the bay with a tiny *Argos* drawn up on the yellow sickle of sand; the whitewashed town with flat red roofs spread around it. Trees closed around me now, myrtle, olive and pine. Big pines that overshadowed the ground in brown lifeless rings. Even the shafts of bright sunlight between the trees seemed cold.

I made to shout her name and something stopped me. Perhaps the stillness, as though the dark trees were watching. A stream ran between them and I knelt to drink. The water was so icy that it cramped my stomach. And while I drank, I had the uneasy feeling of someone watching. Not even birds called, in this dark heavy closeness.

I splashed across the stream, the water icy around my ankles, numbing my toes in the open leather sandals. I found another path that was just faint traces in the rocks, as though generations of feet had worn them smooth. Without knowing why, I followed, and more pines closed around me. Ahead, the stream bubbled from some outlet, the ground thick with pine needles like the shaggy brown hide of a beast.

Up among rocks, where the stream bubbled, was the slit of a cave.

I stopped. Even a peasant boy knows there are places no male goes; special places of the Mother. All I knew about Mother Goddess was not to go near her shrines. This was a dark rocky slit, shaped between outjutting stones. But there were no carvings, no offerings. No long-haired priestess crept out to warn me off.

I remember a crow cawing, as though with black laughter. They are clever birds and know about death. I still do not know why I went forward. I remember my feet making no sound on the shaggy pine floor; the darkness of the stone slit, so close that each cold side touched my body.

Inside was a thicker cold darkness that smelled like the breath of something horrible. It left a sick little taste in my mouth as though the cold air was tainted with something foul. There was just enough light to see how the cave floor sloped to a deep dark pit. And as my eyes grew accustomed to the dark, I saw a tangle of pale objects. Some thin and angled, others round.

I stared at them and they stared back, from eye-sockets black as Hades-underworld; staring, full of the dead grinning life that skulls have.

Dozens of skeletons lay in the pit, perhaps hundreds. In death, a dreadful litter to mock things living. Arm and leg bones, rib cages like splintered barrel-staves. The curved pelvic bones, hand bones with clutching curved finger joints. And picked clean; all through winter the crows and rats must have feasted. The sharp horrible pictures came into my mind like a curse.

I do not know how long I stood there, cold horror crawling on my body. I shut my eyes as I backed out but the hideous images remained clear, the foul taste of death making me retch and vomit. My foot nearly slid on something and I looked down. Not another bone, a corn grinder, fallen from someone's girdle and broken.

I had found the men of Lemnos.

Some things happen like bad dreams. There are parts of the dream you push from memory. Like breaking a wine jar and finding only some of the pieces. I remember the skeletons, the skulls, that horrible tangle of bones. Then my feet on the smooth rock, splashing through the ice-cold water. Dark trees and clear sharp sunlight flashing past because I was running. No noise behind me but a mad yelling coming from my mouth. Blundering through a clump of trees, dripping with moisture. And from their cold shadows came Ixlos, her eyes glittering.

'You found them,' she said.

I nodded. The terror on my face was truth enough.

Her skirt was still tucked in her waist and she let it fall as she spoke again. 'Did you keep goats in your village, Pylos?'

I nodded again. I could not understand the question. Ixlos pressed her lips tight and slipped her hands into her waistbelt.

'They make milk and cheese. Then meat and leather. The wealth of a village; so you pen them to keep the wolves out.' Her voice was very low and calm. 'But what if someone left the goat pen open, Pylos? To let in the wolves.'

'I don't understand.' My own voice strange among these heavy shadows and cold dripping water.

'Pylos, if someone wanted to destroy everything you had, you would fight. Stop them.'

'I don't know,' I answered.

'You do,' she replied calmly, unslipping her belt. 'You would do whatever you had to. So we made a clean sweep.'

A clean sweep. The boys as well, like so many wine jugs. Now her belt was looped like a sling and she ducked to catch up a smooth round stone; her mouth sad and tight, but fixing me with her eyes, she slipped it into the sling and swung it around.

That movement made me duck. The stone took a chip from the tree beside me. It was that fast and hard. I ran on down the hill, three paces, then dived forward. The next stone flew over my head.

'Pylos!' I heard her scream.

I will never know if she was just trying to scare me. A third stone smashed itself on a rock and I ran hard. Perhaps there were more stones but the broken wine jug nightmare closed around me. I do not remember getting back.

The lower slopes were long-grassed hillsides. And there were most of the men, back from hunting; the women around them, most asleep in the sun. Jason sat up, yelling a question. I had the wits to run past, down to where Heracles slept alone. In my panic I kicked him. He sat up, blinking.

'Why did you kick me?' His voice very mild.

I went to my knees, gabbling and pointing. The women had woken, staring at us like cats. Heracles just nodded and stood, pulling me up; shoving me to go back uphill with him. Jason shouted again but Heracles ignored him. None of the heroes thought it worth their dignity to follow.

I think some of the women did. Heracles tramped loudly as we entered the forest but there were other, quieter, sounds. No sign of Ixlos. But even the crows were silent as though sensing a cat-like presence stealing among the pine shadows. I stopped by the cave and that mad yelling note cracked back into my mouth. Heracles hit me, just hard enough to smack sense into my brain. Then he entered the cave.

I followed, terrified, but more scared to be away from him. He looked down at the death pit and those skulls grinned back. We must have been mad to think all the men would sail away. And looking at the skulls, I could see all had a mark. A splintered hole on the forehead or side. Such as a corn grinder would make, swung in the hand of a vengeful woman.

Heracles cleared his throat and sniffed loudly. 'This is a Mother cave, very old. A good place for the bodies.'

They had carried them all this way up the hills. Old men, young men, boys. Some on their backs, some between two or four women, eyes sightless, arms trailing. The women would have chanted their songs, the secret name of Mother Goddess no man knew. The cave lit with mutton-fat lamps; and one by one, the bodies thrown into the pit. They would bloat and rot to putrescence amid the scramble and flutter of forest vermin glutting themselves full. Horrible images made us turn quickly and go outside.

Heracles grabbed some leaves and blew his nose. 'I will never understand women,' he said. Sweat ran over his black-stubbled cheeks. 'I thought something like this had happened.'

'Shall we tell the others?' I asked.

Heracles frowned and spat again, as though that death-taste was still in his mouth. We left the shadow of the pine-belt and stood on the open grassy slopes, under Zeus-given sunlight. Heracles spat a third time and pushed his lips out in a hard smile.

'Half won't believe us. That half will be dead before dawn. Then more killing and the voyage over.'

I wondered why he was speaking so loudly. Then I realized he spoke not to me, but to the unseen women, listening, in the shimmering heat waves, among the long grass — who would hesitate before killing the mighty Heracles and bringing great trouble to their island. He spoke again, as loudly.

'I don't know why they killed their men. That is Mother business. Our voyage must go on and we cannot row if our heads are smashed with corn-pounders.'

He began walking down the hill, even whistling. I jogged beside him, still wobbly-legged. Still that watching cat-like feeling. A wind stirring the grass-tops, making the sweat cold on my face. Heracles spoke softly, these words intended only for me.

'Not a word of this to Jason.'

So we went on down to where the crew were still

gathered. Listening to their chatter was better than the watching silence and the horror of those uplands. But it was no longer normal.

And I did not see Ixlos again.

That evening, Heracles called all our princes and heroes together at the dockside. They came sullenly, guessing what he would say. He asked if they were real champions? The best warriors of Greece unable to voyage more than a week before giving up? Were they so scared of the unknown lands?

The women came also, listening in silence. Queen Hisyphyle sat beside Jason, stiff and formal. Those little corn grinders in her gold headdress made me shudder. Heracles finished by saying he would sail *Argos* alone to the Dardanelle Straits. The Trojans would not harm him; they would be too busy laughing at how the great voyage ended.

Some of the heroes growled. Some sat awkward and silent. But even Zetes, the boaster, had nothing to say. Or Jason. It was old Polyphemus who got to his feet first. He just looked around and nodded. Then Butes got up, Tiphys, Castor and Pollux together. Then the others, shamefaced, not looking at the women, or each other. They knew it was time to go but, like big children, hated to be told.

The women said nothing. I think they were glad because they had their freedom again. And the next generation was safe in their wombs. So we made ready to go and they stocked *Argos* full. Jason might have stayed — Lemnos would have been his kingdom — but he was captain and leader. Heracles was right. But none of them liked him for it.

And when Lemnos fell away, he was the only one who did not look back. Even I wondered if I had left Ixlos with child. A choppy southwesterly swell hit us, streaming our faces with water. Maybe it hid some tears; maybe some of the women who waved goodbye also cried. Maybe.

So we pressed on, our destiny marked deep as writing marks in a clay tablet. It was better on Poseidon's ocean because he was a God we understood, not something dark, old and suffocating. We had the creak of ropes, the flap of the sail; dried olives, salt fish and tough goat-meat. Everyone was soon in better spirits and, after the first day, even Jason smiled.

Ahead lay the Dardanelles and our first battle.

Chapter 5

The Dardanelles — Hellespont — was guarded by the great city of Troy. Each city has a guardian god and the Trojans chose storm-making Poseidon as theirs. The Sea God himself might have shaped those straits.

Their entrance is as close as the slit of that Lemnos cave. Then they open to a long voyage down wild coasts, many days' sailing. At the far end, they close in a fearsome trap that guards the unknown sea itself.

Now the first entrance was before us, through shallow waters that the proud, arrogant Trojans guarded as fiercely as a warrior holds his honour. Their city was protected by high strong walls, walls that were built — the Trojans boasted — by the Gods. And their galleys blocked the trade routes to the unknown seas.

Our crew rowed slowly and spent the day making their weapons ready. None were afraid but even the boldest hunter thinks twice before thrusting his head in the lion's mouth. Only Heracles made no preparations. He slouched at his oar, whistling.

Jason ordered me to clean and sharpen his sword; to polish his bronze helmet with the black horsehair crest. He fitted it on, the cheek flaps framing a tight-lipped face. I made to go and he held me, speaking in a low voice.

'Tell me what you saw on Lemnos.' His words just audible above the creak of oarlocks.

Heracles had told me to say nothing. But Jason

was my captain and if the Trojans caught us, it would not matter. So I told him. We were in the bow, the crew straining their backs before us. Jason heard me out, then nodded and sighed. Perhaps he knew some of it already — or that no kingdom came without a price.

'A man who marries in Lemnos will have to behave himself,' he said.

He smiled and a little of the old Jason returned. Only a little, because the lines of command were already deep in his face. And I think he had not forgiven Heracles for shaming him. So he went back to the stern, buckling on his sword-belt.

Hellespont drew nearer.

We held off from the straits until last daylight. Troy itself was inland and we could not see its high-built walls. And when the setting sun made the overcast clouds crimson and gold, we rowed in. Even then, against sea and distant land, moved dancing black specks. Trojan galleys, which had seen our ship and were moving to block us.

We crept forward. It would take two days to clear the straits but this first night was the most important. And as darkness closed, we rowed hard. A good night to run the straits; gusty winds and choppy seas that would hide our oar-stroke hitting water.

I squatted in the stern, beside Steersman Tiphys and Jason. His lips moved but I do not know which god he prayed to. I wished I could do something more than sit and wait. Our crew strained, the oars splashed. Slowly, black in the dark waters, we moved ahead.

Soon we could hear the trumpets.

The Trojans knew we were there. Their trumpet-calls marked the line of galleys; a deadly brass-tongued noise like howling spears in the night. We rowed and once came a greater splash of oars — a greater blackness swept by like the salt-wet cloak of Poseidon himself. A Trojan galley, missing us in the darkness.

We had the current thrusting against our bows to guide us. And the black tongue of their own trumpets. We wrapped strips of cloth around the oarlocks to muffle them. Slowly, through the darkness, the noise fell behind. There was only the quiet splash of our own oars and the creak of rigging. We rowed hard, in silence, all night and, when morning came, Jason made a noise. He laughed.

There was a mist on the water — like the white concealing arms of a sea nymph. Perhaps Poseidon had decided not to help the Trojans this morning. Gods like to change their minds. Now the men relaxed; there was laughter and handslapping on sweat-stained shoulders. Jason laughed again, softly.

'We have the Gods to thank,' he breathed. 'And our sharp Greek wits.'

Heracles whistled sharply. Others muttered. Jason should not have said that. Gods do not like mortals boasting how clever they are.

They must have been listening. Because no sooner had Jason uttered those words than a metal-tongued hunting call sounded. And from the thinning mist, showed the yellow-beaked prow and painted eyes of a Trojan war galley.

So there was no more backslapping and laughter.

All the crew set grimly to work. Now came only the sound of creaking leather and wood; oars straining in the brackets, the sharp cold splash of their long blades. Fast, but the Trojan galley plunged on behind, with a heavy deliberate speed. They had been resting all night, waiting for an intruder who slipped through the picket line. Now they drew closer.

Splash, splash, splash, like heavy powerful footsteps. The hoarse chanting of their rowers grew louder. And louder.

Our men strained in silence and Jason braced on the stern. He did not look back. Beside him, Tiphys was rock-steady on the steering oars. I dipped barleycakes in watered wine and passed them out. They ate as they rowed, panting now. Only Heracles whistled, bolting his cake with one gulp. And as I turned for the stern, something struck the deck plank with a loud strumming. A bronze-tipped arrow with red-painted shaft and grey goose-feather flights.

Another came, and another. They whistled around us or stuck in the mast. One skinned Castor's knuckles but, like a proper Spartan, he ignored it. Butes was more excitable and when an arrow plucked his sidewhiskers, he yelled loud. 'Hey, Jason, swords and shields now? Let's go down fighting!'

I knew what he meant. Trojans worked their slaves hard — everyone does; that's what slaves are for. Hard work, stinking work. Even sacrifice. Our heroes would die before they let some priest gut them. And our sail faltered, the wind now blocked by the galley behind. Jason glanced back, then suddenly grinned.

'Helmets off! Hide your weapons!' he yelled. 'Look defeated!'

He pulled off his own helmet, tossing it to me. All were battle-wise and understood more quickly than I did. Perhaps this Trojan galley thought we were just another trading ship, chancing a passage. If they knew it was *Argos*, each man a picked warrior, they would stand off and feather us from bow to stern in red-shafted goose-grey death.

I wanted to flinch and duck. I sweated cold as though back in the skeleton cave. The arrows were sleeting around me but I dared not show fear with Jason's quiet gaze on me. But still I flinched as an arrow hit the rail between us.

Behind us, fearsome in black and yellow, came the Trojan galley, painted eyes unblinking as the wave beats splashed up; glaring at the wretched trespassers. The sharp ram-beak cut the water, longing to smash into the wooden sides of *Argos*.

In the bow stood a bronze-clad man, his armour flashing with gold and blue enamel. His bronze helmet seemed polished with morning flame, the long red crest floating behind. He stood, hands on hips, the very picture of arrogant powerful Troy; running down a thief like a lion catching a jackal.

Other men gathered behind their gold-flashing captain. Brown half-naked archers took aim and fired. Their arrows pierced our sail now — their way of teasing us; they wanted us alive because Greek slaves always fetched a good price. Jason smiled grimly, showing his strong white teeth. He gently pushed Tiphys aside and took the steering oars himself.

'Slacken off,' he shouted. 'Pretend you are too tired to row!'

It was almost no pretence. The men did stop rowing,

their oar-beat splashing off. They sat on their benches, heads bowed. Only Heracles sat straight, yawned loudly and went on whistling.

'Bank oars!' shouted Jason loudly.

As he intended, his words carried clearly to the warship looming behind. They had seen our oar-stroke breaking, the long shafts waver timidly. Their prey in disarray and terror, defeated.

The gold-flashing Trojan captain watched calmly. His galley rode up like the cruel war creature it was; ready to swing around and let the ram-beak chop away one side of oars to make us helpless. We were an easy wallowing prey. Our men slumped, Jason sagging on the steering oars in despair. A shout came from the galley's bow.

'Surrender, Greek thieves!'

In a moment they would be alongside. Jason made himself stagger up with an exhausted flap of his hand, bracing his feet on the deck. Suddenly he roared, a real shipmaster's bellow.

'Left bank up! Right bank — strike!'

And they did! Exactly at that moment. Up came the left bank of oars and the right side cut water. Never did the crew show their training better. Like a wily eel, we back-wiggled out from the passing galley. Their own oars cut water as the Trojan captain guessed our intent. His archers ran to the side as Jason bellowed again.

'Left oars forward! Right oars back!'

Our men slapped the tough ash shafts into the white water, knowing they showed their helpless backs to the enemy; knowing the Trojan archers were already running between their own rowers, bending their bows; knowing, as we came around, this was our only chance to be free.

The arrows flew, a hasty ill-timed volley, over our heads or into the sea. Polyphemus cursed as one jabbed his forearm. Jason's cheek ran with blood but he roared, strong as ever.

'Full ahead! Ramming speed!'

It was as though *Argos* herself heard him. She was like a sea-hawk, skimming the short distance. The Trojan archers jumped aside, their oarsmen scattering. A splintering crash — for the first time I heard the dreadful sound of ship meeting ship. We smashed into the Trojan galley, her oars snapping. A last archer was knocked into the sea. Not enough speed for real impact but we cracked her sideplanks and let in the green sea.

'Reverse oars!' yelled Jason.

And we backed, but a wave-swirl took us side-ways. And the Trojan galley, still under power from its other bank of oars, also came around. We crashed alongside, the gold-flashing captain shouting orders. A moment only we locked and a stream of Trojan warriors scrambled over. Then the same chance swirl took us away. Some fell into the sea and the others fought.

A short fight, while it lasted. Our men grabbed their swords, reacting quick and hard like the trained warriors they were. Zetes cut a man at the waist with a loud shout of joy. Castor fought with a broad grin, knuckles streaming blood. Heracles, still mild-faced, battered two and slung them over the side.

The Trojan galley had fallen back, trailing smashed oars like a broken wing. Stumbling, bloody and awkward as the ship rolled, men grappled in knots, shouting, stabbing, swearing. Jason unsheathed his sword as the Trojan captain scrambled up onto the stern, followed by two of his men.

Tiphys met one with a dagger and they closed. Jason clashed with the captain; the third made for me, his eyes glaring under his helmet. I had no idea how to fight. I ducked, he kicked at me, stabbing down with his sword. It jabbed into the deck; he raised it to strike again, then jerked horribly as Heracles' fist slammed against his head. With his eyes rolled white, he went over the side. Heracles was still mild, whistling as he pulled me up.

Tiphys rose, wiping his bloody dagger on the dead Trojan's kilt. Below, the fight was over, the Trojan slain or wounded thrown overboard. And Jason had the gold-flashing captain backed against the stern, sword pricking his bearded throat. His gold helmet rolled on the deck and he glared, angry with shame but already collecting himself.

I knew his type. Noble and arrogant, thinking Trojan gold would buy his freedom, and that next time, he would be the master. But the same god who thinned the sea mist decided otherwise. Castor had not forgotten his skinned knuckles. He burst onto the afterdeck, roaring as only a Spartan can. And, still grinning like a Spartan, he grabbed the Trojan by arm and leg and threw him over the side.

'A gift for you, Sea God Poseidon!'

The man splashed from sight. Castor swung up the gold helmet by its red horsehair crest and threw that over too. Jason looked angry a moment, thinking of the lost ransom. But Heracles nodded solemnly, declaring it a proper thanks-offering; sending a Trojan to the mercy of his own god. And my first battle was over.

I felt shivery and weak as though I had been running hard all day. Heracles slapped my arm and went back to his oar. Jason shouted for the men to take their places. Tiphys grabbed the steering oars, grinning happily at me. We were under way almost at once, and it was over.

Almost over. I looked back. The gold-flashing captain had managed to surface. His long black hair streamed wetly behind him; his galley too distant, his armour already pulling him down; knowing it was his moment to die. He rolled over, pale face upturned, one arm raised to the blue sky. A wave broke over him and he was gone. In an hour, his galley was a toy boat in the distance; if there were other Trojan ships, we did not see them.

So we had won through. Even though the sight of that drowning Trojan stayed with me all day. Jason ordered wine to toast our victory and made me drink some. The men cheered and shouted but my cup clattered on my teeth. Jason saw that too.

'Hey, Pylos,' he said quietly. 'The first time is always hard. Time you learned to use a sword. You'll need it where we're going.'

We were going up the straits. Following the ships that never returned.

Chapter 6

As I said, Hellespont is like a wine flask with a neck at each end. We kept well to the coast and put in to shore each night. Jason gave me a Trojan sword and made me swing, cut and thrust each night till my arms scorched with pain. The heroes joked in tolerant amusement about my skill in cutting firewood but I went on. The next time a warrior came at me, I wanted to be fighting back.

We all thought about the far end of Hellespont and the fearful danger that closed up.

Not even Heracles knew what it was. He had explored this coast by overland trails and knew a little of what we would find. Little cities, petty kingdoms and bandits. No soft beds, good wine and marble palaces for the heroes, he said, blinking mildly. His little taunts were being disliked more and more.

The second night, while I chopped and cut, Heracles asked Hylas to make up another song. About a brave warrior who crushed the green foeman with his mighty backside. Hylas did, sniggering, but nobody laughed. Least of all Telamon, who had accidentally sat on a bed of nettles and would sleep on his stomach tonight. Heracles laughed and Hylas thought himself safe beside his mighty friend. So he strummed his lute and sang, and Telamon glowered.

I just swung my sword. Heracles had never fitted into the crew or even tried to. Nor did he care what the others thought and only Hylas was his friend.

Me, I was a puppy he saved from drowning, that was all. Yes, there was trouble coming, so I swung my sword and tried not to feel the tension.

It came soon. The next day.

Doliones was a small town, set in a good harbour. They aped Greek manners, but any true Greek would have been ashamed of the crowded hovels and drystone walls. We took *Argos* in slowly but their own ships were little more than fishing boats; their town guard as ramshackle as their walls. The ruling merchants were a crafty lot who thought that speaking Greek made them civilized.

Jason was polite though. We needed water and the Doliones readily agreed. The town wells were low, they said, but half an hour from town were good springs. But, they also said, we should go in strength because there were bandits in the hills.

Our heroes scoffed at this. A full crew of warriors just to get water! None of them wanted to go because common labour was beneath them. Jason made them draw lots for a party of ten — and myself. Heracles came too, muttering about getting a new oar to replace his, broken in the Trojan fight.

The road was little more than a track; the hills steep and rocky; spiky thorn bushes and stunted trees. We went in silence and, again, I felt the tension. Not the fear of bandits, but that Heracles was with us. He shambled, kicking stones, looking unconcerned. Somehow that made it worse.

Princes, nobles, warriors, they were sick of his banter. And now wondering aloud just how brave he was. So far he had done no more than anyone. Some

59

said openly, now, that Heracles was an ox for bellowing and a chicken for courage. So far, Jason had stopped any quarrels but Jason was back at Doliones township. Pollux and his twin, Castor, headed this party. They joked loudly about oxen and chickens but Heracles ignored them.

We reached the springs and began to fill the waterskins. The heroes grumbled at having to work and I did most of it. Heracles did not help at all; he wandered around, looking over a small grove of saplings. Pollux threw a waterskin onto the cart and scowled over.

'Heracles!' he yelled. 'I know you've mucked out stables and skinned dead lions. But what about real fighting?' He held up his hand in a boxer's fist.

Heracles blinked at him and belched. He grasped a thick, well-grown sapling and pulled it up from the ground. In such rocky soil, the roots would not have been deep. Pollux cheered and clapped his hands.

'So you've added weeding to your mighty labours. I suppose, in time, that will become a full-size oak with a monster serpent in the branches.'

He and Castor stood grinning. The other heroes were enjoying it too. Heracles just pulled out a knife and began to trim the branches. Castor and Pollux went over and stood watching. Pollux kicked the tree but Heracles just kept working. He began to whistle.

'I think that's a danger sign,' I whispered to old Polyphemus.

He just shrugged. 'The fools are set on their folly.' I think he meant all three of them.

'Heracles,' said Castor. 'Did your mother sleep with one of those giant monkeys from Africa?'

Heracles considered this and shrugged. 'I never asked her. Of course that would be better than a man of Sparta.'

He trimmed the last branch and stood up. Castor and Pollux had stopped grinning. Beside me, Polyphemus sighed, because he knew what would happen now. At least he thought he did.

Because, as Heracles straightened, there came a sudden loud whirring like startled birds; arrows skimming around us, one sticking in Heracles' arm. And a loud shouting, the scramble of men over the top of the ridge.

The bandits had found us. Some hundred of them, escaped slaves, criminals and plain barbarians. Skin-clad, fur-clad, they charged down, waving big hair-covered shields; thinking our little party was an easy target; running straight onto thrusting spears, locked shields and cutting swords. Our heroes broke the charge like a rock breaking a wave. They drew off, regrouping.

Well-armed they were, though. Each with a sword, dagger and throwing spears; also a little axe. And most had bows. Our bowman, Zetes, had not even brought his bowcase. So we formed around the cart and they attacked again, hard, expecting to overcome us this time. Again they ran into locked shields and thrusting spears in the hands of grim skilled warriors.

Jammed between Polyphemus and Castor, their shields covering me, my sword too short to prick a barbarian hide, I glanced back at the one member of our party who took no part in the fighting — Heracles, his face mild, was pulling the arrow from his arm.

61

Now the bandits jeered at us in their strange tongues. They were trying to draw us out. Those with bows arched them, fitting arrows. That was bad. Just a few well-aimed shafts and we would be finished. The first arrows skimmed among us with their ugly hiss. Then came a loud roar; Castor and I were knocked flat.

Heracles had simply charged over us. He had his new oar shaft in both hands and ran straight at the bandits, waving it like a huge club. None of the heroes liked Heracles but still they grouped to help him. Even Castor, scrambling to his feet. Then they paused, because there was no need.

The bandits were thrown aside like skittles. Heracles' arm ran with blood but it did not slow him down. He whirled and he smashed, his eyes glaring red, white spittle on his black-stubbled chin. It is hard to describe how he moved; like a perfect fighter and a perfect dancer, the thick sapling light as a wooden straw; the bandits falling, their weapons clattering. Five down, then ten, fifteen. Panic swirled through them like a storm current and they scattered. They must have thought the furies were among them.

None of us moved to help. We would only have got in the way. And, inside minutes, only bodies were left because Heracles had killed every man he struck. Then he stopped and, like a stain wiped away, the red fury went from his eyes.

His rage was gone, sudden as melted ice. He shrugged and, pulling out his knife, began to clean the sapling of blood and brains. Then he frowned, puzzled, looking over to us.

'Castor, what were we talking about?' he asked.

'I don't remember,' said Castor.

'Neither do I,' said Pollux.

Spartans are the bravest of men. But watching Heracles fight was like seeing the dark rage of destruction itself. Then, his great strength made him unbeatable. So he blinked, and finished cleaning his oar shaft. Polyphemus muttered that the Spartan twins deserved to have their heads broken for trying to pick a fight with Heracles. Now Heracles threw the oar shaft to me.

'Put this in the cart,' he said. 'My new oar.'

The bandits were long gone. We filled the last water-skins in silence. Castor swaggered, and combed his beard with a small ivory comb. Pollux sang a little song about cattle raiding. I think they were relieved that Heracles had forgotten their quarrel. I do not think he forgot. When he threw the staff at me, he winked.

I will never understand Heracles.

I think the Doliones merchants knew the bandits would attack. They were crafty enough for that — hoping our crew would do what their own town guard could not. They gave us gifts of food and saw us off with many fine compliments about our bravery. But fate prodded a dark finger and strong wind came across *Argos* the next day. Evening came and the wind drove us to a beach. We went ashore.

We had scarcely lit our fires when the clank and rush of armoured men came across the pebbly shoreline. More bandits? So we met them, the full crew, and were soon tripping on their dead bodies. They gave back, moonlight shone on an upturned face and Jason yelled to stop the fight.

We were fighting the Doliones townspeople, who thought we were pirates. My own sword was sticky with blood; I had wrenched my wrist painfully as I thrust it into someone's body.

We helped them burn their dead. And we put to sea with the black smoke of the funeral pyre drifting into the blue sky.

'They wanted us to fight their enemies,' said Jason beside me. 'The Gods punished them by making them fight us.'

So our first contact on this unknown shore ended in blood. Much later I heard the story from a bard. By then the many-weaponed bandits had become six-armed monsters. They were not. And the Doliones should have fought their own battles. Then, the black funeral smoke would not have risen.

But the Gods played with us and we would soon find out how cruel their sport was.

Then the weather closed in. For a week we struggled, our sail furled against the contrary wind, crawling with oars from one beach to the next; and for two long weeks, pinned on the coast of a peninsula. Oars alone could make no headway. So we drew up *Argos*, cut poles to put the sail over them as shelter. And we waited.

The shore was wild and rocky, the low hills covered with thick thorn bushes and stunted little trees. A galley is uncomfortable at the best of times; soon the crew were muttering about bad voyage luck. Even Heracles became surly.

Everyone began looking hard at Mopsus, our seer. He had only pulled an oar so far — a cross-eyed man is useless in fighting because he sometimes hits his friends. And if prophets cannot stop bad luck, they tend to have some of their own. Like being left behind, or even thrown overboard.

I was watching our heroes now. Putting up with discomfort was one thing; thinking the Gods were angry was another. Their sense of self-importance suffered because they were supposed to be specially loved by the Gods; or even related to them. Mopsus began looking uneasy and I do not blame him. It would have been a long walk home.

Then, on the twelfth day, he woke us with a screech. A kingfisher, he said, had fluttered over Jason's head. On this morning the winds were lessening and Mopsus said we must sacrifice to the Gods now, and the wind would change.

So we made our way up those thorny slopes to higher ground; more bare rocks and little streams gushing around them. At the highest place we built an altar, said the right prayers and sacrificed a goat — caught with much trouble. That should have been enough, but as we turned to go, a voice bellowed. Heracles.

'Mopsus, aren't you forgetting something? These are old lands, Mother lands. Rhea, Cybele, whatever she calls herself. We should sacrifice to her too.'

Mopsus licked his lips and looked uneasy. 'I am not sure that is necessary,' he said. 'The omens —'

Heracles hooted with laughter. 'A kingfisher looking for breakfast? She will send a worse sign than that. Maybe our skeletons will fill a cave. None of these brave heroes want that, do they?'

He grinned and cracked his knuckles. There were

loud angry mutters now but Jason kept his face smooth. He ordered another goat caught, with much more trouble, and Mopsus made a Mother image with vines. So we sacrificed again, with more prayers to Rhea-Mother. There were set faces though. Heracles had made our heroes feel like naughty boys caught stealing apples.

Maybe it was right to please the Mother. A spring gushed from the rocks as we made our way down, and Mopsus screeched that that was a good omen. All the streams were in flood on the way back down, tumbling the bodies of small animals, drowned, from their lairs. Mopsus said that was a good omen too. He stubbed his toe painfully crossing a stream and Heracles asked if that was a sign from the Gods as well. Mopsus just snarled.

He looked relieved too. Because the very next morning, the winds were blowing in the right direction. So his reputation was restored. Although any fisherman could have told them that calm and wind-change come after bad weather. I am sure Mopsus knew that too and just waited for the right moment. A kingfisher, a kite or a dolphin; a crafty seer can make anything into an omen. He handled our heroes like big children.

But when Heracles prodded him to sacrifice to Earth Mother Rhea, that was different. Maybe Heracles knew it was a trick. But he should not have invoked her name. Or used it so lightly; or to jeer at our heroes and shame them. But Heracles was sometimes like a blindfolded man running along a clifftop. Sooner or later the man must fall.

And that is what happened.

Chapter 7

Now a calm descended. As though Mother Goddess herself smoothed the water with a swish of her kirtle. So our heroes rowed and now the sun blazed hot. Around the peninsula lay more endless wild coast, where the tangled forest grew down to the waterline. And unknown birds called with shrill high cries like the laughter of mocking women.

Our heroes rowed on, held by their pride. All day the oar-beat slapped water, all the next day. Nobody faltered or stopped, because that is the way with heroes. They always have to push themselves, even though pride can break. And on the third day, it did.

We put to sea at first light. I sat in the bows, watching for rocks. My arms were aching less from the sword-play now. And, splash-splash-splash, we rowed from the pink half-light of dawn to noon. Often we sang a rowing song, shouting 'stroke, stroke!' Not this day. The only sound above the ship-noise was Heracles' maddening shrill whistle — his face mild, his lips pursed — mocking his shipmates as much as those bird calls did.

We always stopped at noon for barleycakes, olives and watered wine. But not today. When Jason called halt, the heroes kept rowing and Heracles kept whistling. Noon, the sun hammering the water like a blacksmith, beating it to shimmering fire. So we rowed into afternoon, one hour, two, then the first rower collapsed over his oar. Butes, who was always better at finding honey. Without words, sensing the mood, Jason took his place.

Those oar shafts were long and thick. A man had to grip them tightly, lean forward, then pull back with all his strength. And when the oar splashed and the ship moved that tiny inch forward, he had to do it again. And again. The sun hammering like bandy-legged Heiphaistos, Blacksmith God; the water molten, the sun blasting like a furnace. Another rower collapsed and there were groans now, gasps from the others.

Heracles still whistled, not even out of breath.

Sweat glistened on all the straining bodies. The bronze-fire sun grew in heat and the stink of melting pitch rose from the deck-planks. On and on, the sun pounding now like ten bronze hammers. The waters still a dull sheen like stretched linen. Sweat-stench and pitch-smell mingled together.

The splash of oars went on and on.

Another man went over. Then another and another, gasping, their strength gone. Heracles just whistled.

The splash-beat of oars now mixed with the groans of straining men. And that shrill tuneless whistle.

There were no rocks in this water. Crouched in the bows, I felt of less use than the weed growth on the hull. But I sensed also this was not just about rowing. It was the crew, pitting themselves against Heracles. And more fell out. Old Polyphemus, his beard bloody where he had bitten his lips. Telamon and then Orpheus, crashing in a dead faint.

Now the rowing became jagged and *Argos* wavered. Now even the strongest were going. Calais, then Zetes. The rowing pace slowed. More men went over and soon only four remained. Jason, Castor, Pollux and Heracles. The first three were gasping, shuddering, only their honour holding them now. Heracles was red-faced, puffing a little, but still whistling — even glancing about as though bored.

Castor went first. He was better at taming horses, anyway. Then Pollux, on his knees; still holding the oar in his tight boxer's grip. And minutes, straining creaking minutes later, Jason went down too. The sweat streamed on their bodies like that fresh spring on the Mother Goddess mountain. The sun hammered and hammered.

One oarlock still creaked though. To the sound of whistling.

Heracles should have stopped then. But on his flat stubbly face was a blank stubborn look. He whistled and he rowed. Now he was moving the ship sideways and Tiphys had to struggle to hold it on course. Heracles had won. He should have stopped. But he did not think like ordinary people — or even like a hero. He was Heracles, the strongest man in the world. Even Tiphys was straining when a snapping sound cracked over the glassy waters. Heracles' oar had broken again. He muttered in disgust and threw the broken pieces away. Then he pursed his lips and whistled.

Late afternoon. Just enough of a breeze to drift us into a little cove. The crew had recovered just enough to pull *Argos* up onto the beach, then collapsed again. I made big driftwood fires and prepared food. Salt fish, cheese, olives and the last jar of onion relish to spread on our bread. But the men ate silently, moodily, because they had been bested, all of them. Even Jason did not smile.

And there was worse to come.

I have said before I did not understand Heracles. Never less than now. Because he ate a huge meal, then nudged Hylas for a song. And that shallow comic young man obliged. Songs about heroes who fought their ashwood oars and lost; whose boasting alone should have filled our sail with a hurricane blast.

Hylas forgot he was among the first to fall over. He sang, plucking his lute. And Heracles beat time, hand smacking his own thigh, roaring with laughter. And, even now, I did not think he did it to hurt the crew — only to amuse himself, because the strongest man in the world does not have to care who he hurts.

It seemed his laughter went on all night. I rolled up in my blanket and tried to shut out the sound. Polyphemus, near me, pulled his beard. 'The strongest man and the biggest fool,' he growled and went to sleep.

When I woke, the fires were grey ash and blackened sticks.

That was unusual. Heroes do not like doing chores and normally I was prodded awake much earlier. Most of the men were awake, sitting in small groups, eating bread and olives. That was unusual too. Heroes like to be served their meals. So I made up the fires, looking around.

Jason was missing. So were Castor and Pollux, Calais and even Zetes, who normally had to be kicked awake. Butes said they had gone looking for water and firewood. Heroes, doing my chores? I said nothing but a strange prickle of unease came over me.

Heracles was gone too. Hylas was still asleep, but he woke up, saw the grim looks and remembered his comic songs of the night before. He bounded off, looking for Heracles. Polyphemus wandered off too, looking for mushrooms, a great favourite of his. My unease prickled and I thought I would look for Jason. Tiphys touched my ankle as I passed.

'Don't go wandering, boy. You'll get lost.'

'Just to the top of the hill,' I said.

He shrugged and I went. But I was thinking about what he said — and the way he said it. Heroes did not concern themselves with the ship's boy. That prickling unease came over me again. And down the beach, Mopsus sat on his own, his clothes and hair streaked with ash from the fire. He was casting little bones and looking at the pattern they made.

I went up the hill and soon wished I had not. There were straggling clumps of trees and deep cold pools of water. Unpleasant traces of the Mother forest on Lemnos; some of the pines fallen, covered with vine like stealing green fingers; clumps of laurel too, becoming thicker as I went up. Then, with a rustle, the branches parted and someone came out.

Zetes.

He glared at me in a blank unseeing way. His beard straggled damply as though he had been sweating. His hair clung to his forehead in sticky wet streaks. Beyond the laurel clump was a gully; a single fallen brown pine lay across it. Other men were there.

71

Castor and Pollux. Calais … and Jason. They sat rigidly, the silence as cold as the shadows. Nobody looked at me, the intruding peasant boy. Castor and Pollux were damp and sweaty too, and Jason's big loose grin entirely gone. He looked at me. Then a howl came, but not from their tight-shut lips. It swelled around them like the bellow of an earthquake.

It came from the end of the gully, where there was another of those deep cold pools. Beside it sprawled a limp white figure, whose head and shoulders were in the dark water. Beside it crouched Heracles, his thick body bunched in the old lionskin. He beat his hands so hard on the rock that it seemed the stone would break. He howled again, this time the painful loud noise drew out to a name.

'H — H — Hylasss …!!'

It was clear what had happened. Hylas had knelt to drink, slipped and banged his head; fallen into the water and drowned. A cousin of mine slipped in a tidepool just like that. But Heracles was in a frenzy, battering the stones so hard that his hands were already red. He pulled up the body, glaring up at us, insane, blank and full of pain.

'HHHHH … YYY … LL … AAASSSS'

'The madness is on him,' said Jason quietly.

Already they were scrambling back and I followed. They ran in a curious way, like naughty children. The laurel rustled around them. Heracles howled again and it sounded closer. I ran faster and so did the others.

We slipped down the hill, setting the rocks tumbling, faster and faster as the howling sounded closer. Like the time I ran from the Lemnos cave, the same shimmer-feeling of cold unreal fear on my body. Only once I looked back, nearly falling as I did. Heracles was staggering after us, Hylas limp across his shoulder like a long white fish.

'HHHYY … LLL … AASSS!'

We scrambled down to the beach. Perhaps the crew had already heard Heracles howling. Because *Argos* was back in the water, the other heroes in place on the rowing benches. But nobody asked questions as we splashed on board. Tiphys took his place on the steering oar and we pushed off.

I was at the bows, glancing back once. Rowing benches empty, Hylas and Heracles — and one more. Polyphemus.

'Polyphemus!' I shouted.

The heroes had already noticed. Even Jason, but he still shouted orders to Tiphys. *Argos* backed out, oar-beat splashing. I turned again and saw something awful. Heracles, pounding along the foreshore, the limp white form aslung his shoulder, spray drenching them both. His mad shouts deafened us like the thunder of Earth-shaking Poseidon himself.

'HHH … YYY LLLLAAASSS …'

But the oar-beat faltered. Polyphemus was still ashore and some even muttered that we should not leave Hercules like this. Some men stopped rowing but Jason ran between the benches, raising his hand. 'Heracles is mad!' he yelled. 'The hand of the Earth Mother is upon him!'

And quickly, Zetes, both hands on his oars, his face still shiny and red, cried, 'We have a long voyage — too long with that madman on board!'

Calais, beside him, rose a moment, shouting around, 'His madness will destroy us all!'

'Polyphemus ...' I said again.

I did not shout the words. Not that it mattered. The splash of oars was louder; so were the howls from the headland. Heracles was running, splashing a sharp white furrow of surf, waist-deep into the water. Then to his armpits and black-stubbled chin. But the ocean was stronger, much stronger even than Heracles. Our oars splashing, like the slap of Poseidon's own hand, we drew away.

So we drew away. Everyone knew we could never let Heracles back on board. Nobody mentioned Polyphemus. I glanced back from the bows and saw him on the headland. Lonely and distant. The wind brought a single faraway shout from him and he flung something over the cliff. The mushrooms he had gone to collect.

It must have showed on my face. Jason came up and stood beside me. He was still breathing hard after that mad scramble, his voice hoarse.

'Pylos. You, most of all, are here because of Heracles. But there are things you do not understand. Perhaps one day you will.'

Then he turned, raising his voice in a rowing chant and the crew answered. Stroke! Stroke! Their hoarse chanting drowned out all thought. And questions. *Argos* gathered speed and soon that coast and headland were lost from view. That night we pulled up at another cove and went ashore. We made the fires, we ate and slept. Nobody mentioned Heracles or Hylas. Or Polyphemus.

I thought about them, though — wrapped in my

blanket and still shivering. Was Heracles left behind because nobody could control him? Or perhaps his own words caught up with him; we had not given enough to the Mother. So now she had Hylas, even Polyphemus and Heracles.

The next morning, it was as though nothing had happened. The men took their places, there were jokes, rude remarks, the usual banter to Steersman Tiphys about the soft job he had. They settled quickly, like equals now because there was no Heracles. Pollux raised his voice in a song about how great were the Spartans.

Even in this short time, they had recovered. And that was good, because another headland and a little city lay before us. This one with only a wooden palisade, not even drystone walls and no half-Greek merchants pretending they were civilized. They were enemies; they would fight; for one of our crew, that was good.

Pollux, the Spartan boxer who nobody could beat.

Chapter 8

This harbour was shallow and filthy with litter. Behind the log walls, the roofs of this 'city' were simple brushwood. The gate arch was stone, so Greeks had come this far across the overland trails. We were short of water but armed warriors clustered on the foreshore. Jason backed oars. Fighting would only reduce our strength. It was better to go thirsty.

And these warriors looked true barbarians — long trailing moustaches, blue tattoo marks on either cheek. Their leather armour was set with horn plates, their high-pointed helmets of leather.

Their king — if he deserved such a title, muttered Jason — waded into the shallows. A thickset man with a smashed nose and fists like knotted oak roots. His long moustaches hung to his waist and were tucked in his belt.

'Hey, Greeks! Want water and food?' He showed a crude understanding of our language. 'But the first man ashore has to fight me!'

One of our oars missed a stroke. It was Pollux, sitting upright and open-mouthed. Pollux had always wanted to prove himself the best fighter on the ship. Jason yelled for silence, but too late. Castor stood up and shouted.

'A fight with bare fists? That's all?'

'That's all!' shouted the big-nosed bully.

He swaggered, grinning, hands on hips. He had all his front teeth and that was a bad sign. Even

Pollux had two knocked out. But he laughed, seeming comical, like the simple barbarian he was. So Jason nodded and we took *Argos* in to the shore. Their full assembly of warriors did not much outnumber us.

But our crew were careful. They waded ashore in full armour, shields and spears. The king — Amycus was his name — waved his warriors back. I did not like that little piggy glint in his eyes or even the hoarse cajoling note in his voice. He reminded me of Thegus. He shouted again, mocking.

'Hey, Greeks, armour and weapons? All I want is a fair fight.'

He threw off his armour. Underneath he wore a sleeveless horsehide vest. His arms bulged with thick blue-tattooed muscle. With thick leather braces on each wrist, his knuckles scarred and broken, more and more he reminded me of Thegus.

His men were grumbling little battle songs, like the rough savages they were. We would beat them in a fight, but enough of our rowing benches were empty already. More, and *Argos* would not have the oar-power to fight the currents ahead. Amycus knew this too. He roared again, hands on hips.

'Fight me! If you lose, then we have your armour and weapons. Anything else of value!'

Our crew muttered. Even Jason stood silent a moment. Long enough for someone else to elbow his way to the front. Pollux.

'I'll fight you,' he said. As mild as Heracles. 'But I'm weak from rowing. So, just a knock-down?'

He threw off his helmet and undid the straps of his armour. He even yawned and grinned like an idiot. Spartans are dense but beware of one who plays the fool. Even Pollux, whose big round face made him look foolish anyway.

Amycus thought so. His piggy eyes glinted; he showed yellow teeth under the long black moustaches. His voice was as hard as the muscles under his brown tattooed skin.

'Just a knock-down. That's all.'

Pollux removed his armour; his twin knelt to take off the leg-greaves. Amycus stepped back and one of his men threw two strips of rawhide leather at Pollux. Amycus was binding his own fists with rawhide. This was no simple knock-down. Rawhide meant broken bones, blood. Amycus was a bully and, like all bullies, had to go on proving himself.

The fight began quickly. Pollux stripped to his kilt, wrapped his hands in the rawhide and ambled up slowly. Like a clumsy-footed shepherd with a big innocent grin.

'Ready,' he said.

Amycus grinned back like a big savage bear. He shuffled, then threw a sudden strong punch like a battering ram. Pollux moved his head, looking as though he had stumbled awkwardly. Amycus recovered his balance and punched again with killing speed. Pollux shambled sideways and knelt quickly, pretending to do up his sandal.

'Are we fighting now?' he asked.

He shambled backwards with a big foolish grin. Our men laughed. Amycus followed — with more caution. Their leather sandals clattered on the beach as they circled. Another punch and Pollux ducked again — not quick enough it seemed, the blow landing on his shoulder. But it only threw him around and, as Amycus thundered past, he grabbed the copper comb from his head.

'May I borrow this?' he said pleasantly, and ran it through his own hair. 'Thank you.'

Our men laughed again, even some of his. Amycus knew exactly what Pollux was doing — getting him annoyed so he would fight more rashly. But he was annoyed and in his bloodshot eyes was the doubt of knowing he fought someone stronger. So he did become more impatient to end it. He ran forward, black hair straggling over his burning eyes. Even hasty and angry, he was a deadly fighter; Pollux knew he had risked enough clowning.

It was over quickly then. I was glad of that. Even when you kill a pig, you do it without fuss. Amycus could not retreat into the shelter of his warriors either; a king cannot do that. He came forward, fists bunched hard so that the muscles ran up his forearm like taut ropes around a mast.

A quick exchange of blows. Amycus spat out a tooth and fought on. His own fist smashed into Pollux's eye, Pollux spun like a dancer. Another punch, hard, behind Amycus's ear. Amycus stumbled on but they were the steps of a dead man. One foot caught in a tangle of seaweed and he pitched forward. The sandflies flew up around his face and one settled on a staring eyeball. He did not blink. He was dead.

I did not know what to think. Heracles would have blinked, refusing to fight the man. Pollux, as a hero, picked a fight and killed. Heracles would not have killed because he did not have to. There was a difference here I could not understand. But while they fought, Jason marshalled us into a fighting line. But there was no fight in Amycus's men.

'Go on, Greeks!' This from one with long white moustaches, the tears running down his cheeks. 'Take what you want and go!'

Amycus may have been a bully. But he was a good bully to them and they would not fight us without a chief. So we filled our waterskins, took some of their goats and put off. The wind filled our sail and the heroes cheered lustily. That evening, we put in to another cove and roasted the goats. Jason gave Pollux the best cuts and he ate them grinning, the grease running over his bruised hands. Everyone ate, drank and was happy. There was no Heracles to shame them. No Hylas to make up comic songs. And Polyphemus seemed forgotten.

I was thinking strange thoughts though for a ship's boy, even one half-grown to manhood. If a ship put in to our village and killed our leader, we would be frightened. So what did the people of these lands think of us? Not a civilized crew of heroes, that was for sure. I had to remember Amycus called us ashore. And that other dangers waited, including the most terrible.

The one that blocked our passage to the unknown seas.

I have heard fantastic stories about our voyage — none closer to the truth than an egg looks like a hen. But they are good stories for the bards who get their living that way. Much later I heard a good one about our next stop. It was, sang the bard, the home of a great prophet named Phineus.

But this Phineus, said the story, was plagued by monster winged woman-birds — sent by the Gods because he saw too deeply into the future. So he was blinded and these woman-birds, called Harpies, always snatched his food. They were defeated because we had two fabled heroes among us; Calais and Zetes, winged sons of the North Wind, defeated them.

That is what the bards sing.

Calais and Zetes were big amiable men with mops of black curly hair. Both were fast runners, Calais a great drinker and Zetes a womaniser. I never saw wings on either of them. Sons of the North Wind they might have been, but nobody ever asked who their father was; bastards are touchy about their birth.

And I think old Phineus was a fraud like most prophets. His village was inside a small bay, shallow and rocky. Not much of a kingdom but then Phineus was not much of a prophet. He probably fled here after making one wrong forecast too many.

He was a thin man with very bad teeth and a straggly white beard. He was bald, with pointed ears; his eyes inflamed and half-blind by the bad dust-winds. The headland over the village was full of birds and their droppings were everywhere, including on his ragged smelly clothes. He lived here with a priestess-wife and two daughters. All the villagers thought themselves very lucky that such a great man had come to live among them.

Jason had stopped because this village was a crossroads for travellers. Phineus would know a lot about our journey ahead and even the great danger that guarded the other end of the straits.

Phineus said he would help. He boasted about knowing every stone, rock and tree of the coast ahead. But first (prophets always make conditions) we had to help him. The birds who pestered him in their shrieking snapping clouds; *Argos* must drive them off because the locals were too idle, he said. We were annoyed but agreed to spend a week doing this.

The real problems were hawks and kites; that was Phineus' own fault. He sacrificed for the locals (knowing how to scare them) and the strewn reeking guts and offal attracted the scavengers. The heroes drew straws for nest-wrecking and the 'North Wind' brothers drew the short straws. They did not fly after the birds, but their arrows did.

After a week of this, Jason wanted results. I was with him when he stalked up to Phineus. He reminded the quaking old fraud that there were worse things than scavenging birds. Such as a crew of fifty angry heroes who could do a lot of damage. And Phineus would find out how much damage, unless he told them what lay ahead. What was the fearsome menace guarding the unknown sea?

Phineus quaked a little more, cleared his throat, and told us.

Chapter 9

Yes. He knew what that fearsome danger was. Phineus sat us down before his tumbledown shrine, with its smoke-blackened walls; his big-bellied wife beside him, her hair in long greasy braids. She was adorned with a clutter of brooches, rings and hair-pins, all taken from the local women. She nodded at everything he said, looking as though she had been chewing on those tree leaves that give you funny thoughts.

Phineus told us what the unknown menace was.

Two great rocks guarded the other end of the straits. They were the size of small mountains and moved with a horrible life of their own. The current ran so strongly through them that, even when they were apart, no ship could make headway. And, once a ship was trapped, the grinding rocks crushed it and its crew.

And if we got through, said Phineus, adding that nobody ever had — Phineus rolled his eyes whitely into his head and pulled at his straggly beard — and if we got through, and nobody ever had, then a fearsome array of tribal kingdoms lay ahead before we reached the golden kingdom of Colchis.

Jason asked if Phineus could tell us anything about Colchis. He rolled his eyes whitely again and shook his head. If he told us more, the Gods would punish him dreadfully. Meaning that he did not know, the old fraud.

The next morning we took our leave. A good wind quickly cleaned away the stink of the place. And I knew the hawks and kites would soon be back, so I grinned. Let Phineus explain that to the villagers. Most of the crew were frowning though, thinking about those clashing rocks. Jason noticed my grin, just as he noticed everything. He sat beside me on the stern.

'Hey, Pylos, don't you believe Phineus?'

I thought carefully about my answer. 'I'm from a poor village. We had a prophet once who took everything and made up double-meaning stories.'

Jason laughed. 'So you threw him out, eh? Pelted him with fish heads?'

'No,' I replied. 'Fish heads make a good stew. We pelted him with rocks and goat droppings.'

Jason laughed and went to the bow.

On the steering oars beside me, Tiphys grinned. 'Nobody much believed him, but we do need to know where we are going.'

'Monster rocks that crush every ship?' I asked.

Tiphys's grin faded a little as he strained. 'I hope that much is a lie.'

The 'Clashing Rocks' lay six days up the coast. Enough time for the crew to mutter and think about his other strange tales. That along the unknown sea were thick forests, shores of black sand and savage natives. And far up the end, even stranger lands.

Seas of grass, as huge as our own ocean; on those grassland seas, hordes of nomads who lived on horseback and drank the blood of their mares. Merciless, barbaric and always wandering. Rivers running with gold but, to them, gold had no value.

Animal worship, devils and dragon-snakes all lay beyond the rocks that nobody had passed.

In those six days Jason kept our spirits up. 'We expected dangers, yes?' Grinning, slapping shoulders, his leather cap tilted sideways. 'Rivers of gold that nobody wants?' That made them grin back, because princes and heroes love gold. 'And I never saw rocks that a Greek could not sail past!'

So they cheered and, on the sixth day, wine was passed around. By now the strait was closing in like the sides of a bottle towards the stopper. The next morning we could see the rocks and forest of the other shore. No sign of human life as we put to sea, but we could see bones; the wooden bones of wrecked ships. No sign of the crews, though. Their bones would not float.

Now a shore mist came down, close and thick like white masses of thick wet hair. So we slowed the oar-beat to a crawl and Tiphys sniffed as though he could smell the rocks ahead. Once, the carved prow of a wrecked ship grinned at us.

Now, through the thick whiteness, came a thunderous scraping sound like giant stone teeth grinding together, a stone ogre, rock club in hand, waiting for us. The grinding sound grew closer, louder. Then the mist cleared and for a moment, I wished it had been an ogre.

Because Phineus, the old fraud, had spoken the truth.

There were huge rocks there, monster rocks. I had heard stories about floating mountains of ice. But these were not; they just shook and rumbled as though throttled in Poseidon's own grip. They quivered like a winded horse, little rockslides running like stone trickles of sweat. They did not grind, as Phineus said, but shuddered and heaved as though wanting to. And the water foamed white and shallow between them, breaking against the black teeth of more rocks.

This truth was worse than lies.

'Gods! Zeus, Poseidon, Hera, Athena to whom I have always prayed! You alone can get us through! If it is your will, then we will make this passage. If not —'

Jason broke off, the white foam wet on his lips. He was shouting at the top of his voice to be heard. And he took the steering oars. Tiphys was glad enough to let him. For this, the most dangerous part, the captain must take command. And throw all our lives into the hands of our Gods; all of us, in the long wooden shell of *Argos*. And all the crew, myself included, roared the answer.

'Let oars splash water. Stroke!'

Now the thunder of surf was loud. A louder crashing as more rocks tumbled down. The ship bucked and the spray stabbed like the sharp jabbing claws of a witch woman. I was braced on the stern. Jason kicked a little wicker box that Phineus had given him across the deck at me.

'Open that when I tell you!' he snapped.

Closer now. Running at flood into those massive white arms of surf, the heavy boulders crashing the spray like white teeth. All of us were soaking wet, the heroes straining at their oars, and Jason's face was set with a fierce joy because Gods, fate and life, all fought.

Closer.

We were in the current now. The sides shuddered, split and cracked into rockfalls. Now *Argos* bucked and our crew strained. They had rowed for this moment, for this impact; a powerful ship to force the passage.

'Right oar bank — up!' screamed Jason.

He had seen the danger just in time. A flurry of rocks crashed down. *Argos* turned. Jason wrenched on the steering oars. I was flung up, I grabbed the left oar and together we strained. *Argos* came about, the spray flailing like claws, the green waves crashing down. We strained, my muscles cracked, Jason yelled.

'Oars down!'

We bucked now on a bigger wave, more rocks crashing from the other side, splashing like the thunderbolts of Zeus around us. We were in the middle; the power of the seas, of the land force that shook them, pounded *Argos* like a toy boat. Jason, hauling on the oars, streaming wet, yelled above the fierce thunder.

'The box — now!'

I grabbed it, slipped the catch and threw back the lid. Of all things, a white dove. It fluttered, then flapped upward, into the spray ahead, seeking the clearest air away from the mist.

I heard Jason roaring to me, to the crew.

'There, heroes! Where a dove goes, Greeks can follow!'

Argos shuddered from bow to stern. The rock slides crashed on either side and scraped under our keel. Another thunderous crash and suddenly the foaming white waves were our friends, pushing us through the straits. Tiphys was yelling that he could see Athena's white hand gripping our stern and holding us safe. The black rocks fell behind, the white waves crashed a final time. Oar shafts snapped, the ship ground over a last rock shelf — and suddenly, fast as though a white hand guided us, we bucketed into calmer water.

Not unhurt though. Jason cracked his rib against the oar. Zetes was unconscious, his snapping oar catching him under the chin like an uppercut. Castor's forehead had been grazed by a flying rock. But all of us, although stunned and numb, were grinning, Jason grinning broader than any of us. Because *Argos*, his ship, had survived its greatest passage so far. The thundering growl of rocks and the crash of white foam fell behind us.

Now we slid into calm water with our broken oars. Ahead, the sky was blue and the wild green shoreline opened out again. The new ocean stretched unknown and full of wonder, ahead of us. A fluttering white speck led the way; our dove, released and seeking clear water that *Argos* could follow, now flying onward into the opening great blue waters ahead.

Argos, like the dove, moved into the great unknown sea.

Part Two

The winged golden ram took Prixus to Colchis. There he made a new life. He married the daughter of the king and sacrificed the golden ram as thanks for the flight.

The Golden Fleece was enshrined, so precious that a monster dragon was set to guard it. Sleepless, it guarded the shrine day and night. And still does.

There in Colchis, the Golden Fleece awaits. It is the birthright of all Greeks. Only a true prince of Icolos could fetch the Fleece and take it back. And only then could he claim the kingdom of Pelias as his own.

Chapter 10

Jason took us ashore at the first beach we found. We had need of rest. We relaxed, ate and drank, and while we did, he told us more about our expedition, the part of the story that only mattered if we survived the Clashing Rocks.

He told us for another reason too. Our crew of heroes had braved the utmost danger. Colchis was still distant and meant nothing to them. There were murmurs about returning now, basking in the glory they would receive. Jason knew this and, in the warm late sunlight, told us what Phineus had told him — of Prixus and Hellas; of the Golden Fleece in Colchis.

There was silence when he finished, then a few snorts. Princes and heroes liked a good story, but they had never heard of a sheep with wings, or with a golden fleece.

Telamon spoke first, the son of a king and knowing the ways of kings. 'Jason, that is a fine story. But we have braved the unknown sea. We also know you would like to take Pelias's kingdom from him; that is why he sent you so far. The Golden Fleece does not exist.'

'Phineus said that it did,' replied Jason.

There was silence. We all knew Jason had had long private talks with Phineus. The old fraud had long ears and might have heard tales. Or was Jason making it up? Zetes glowered and Calais spat. Even Tiphys looked uncertain. Jason's lazy sea-dark eyes scanned them all. He spoke slowly and easily, knowing this was as great a challenge as the Clashing Rocks.

'We know this sea is full of fish, the shores full of timber. But Colchis is a land of gold — and further, much further, than any Greek has gone. If we return with a cargo of gold, nobody will doubt us.'

'If we do not choose to follow?' asked Butes.

'Each man must make that decision,' replied Jason, his dark eyes still scanning us. 'But I will go on.'

His lips closed tight. He had nearly said 'alone.' But Jason had been alone all his life. He could not say the word. And he could not appeal. So there was silence. I could hear the snap and creak of rigging on *Argos*, another snort from Zetes, pebbles clattering underfoot as I stood up. I had nothing to go back to, either.

'I will go with you, Jason.'

Princes, nobles, warriors, they all gaped. We had sailed months together but, I think, this was the first time they had noticed me, a peasant boy who stood up first. So all their noble and warrior pride decided what came next. Castor stood up, then Pollux, Tiphys, Zetes, Calais. Then Butes, quickly, before the rest rose in a scramble.

They did not know what would happen at Colchis. But they did fear the stories of how Jason and a ship's boy went where warriors dared not. Those things I learned later. Right then, I just glowed at Jason's look, his smile broadening before he swung around and raised his fist.

'To Colchis!'

'Colchis!' roared the heroes back.

What else could they say?

Long long miles of strange coastline. Long hours of rowing and we soon learned that this sea was as tricky as the straits, with back-eddies that could turn a ship around; wind and squalls, twin sisters to those who lashed so sharply before. These waters were a different green-dark colour, so full of fish that the heroes grew tired of them and preferred their salt herring. Heroes are like big children. I have said this and will say it again.

I had grown half a handspan since the voyage began. Now I took my part at rowing and soon wished I had not. After an hour, my hands and buttocks were raw; after two hours my lungs felt enclosed in bronze pincers. After three, my backbone was breaking and I slumped. Butes, my rowing partner, rubbed salt and water into my wounds; he said it would harden them. It made me yelp with pain and the others laughed. Orpheus sang about the lost maidenhood of my tender hands; Zetes' jokes were a lot ruder.

I rowed on though; past the hurt of hands and backside; learning how to breathe properly and put my full weight on the oar. A week passed, two weeks, and I could row the day through, even though I staggered ashore with all my joints and muscles afire like melting bronze. I still made up the fires and cooked the meals. The heroes let me but now, when I served the food, there were grunts, even a nod or two of thanks.

Up the coast we went. More coast, snaking endless and green ahead. Onwards we sailed, our prow cutting through shoals of silver fish. Our oar beat slapped them out of the water. It was only to the land we looked for danger, remembering the wild stories Phineus had told, and the first milestone of legend.

We passed a broad river, then a high black cape. Another river, Phyllis it was called, as the legends and Phineus told us. Here we rested on our oars and watched; this was where Prixus and the ram had rested on their way to Colchis. Then we laboured on, like oxen at the plough. The next day, Mopsus screeched and pointed. He claimed to have seen a vision of Golden Bowman Apollo in the sky. So we landed, built an altar and sacrificed. It was good to feel the power of our own Gods in this strange land.

We needed their power, we needed their strong hold, as we ventured further.

At another fortress town behind a wooden wall, leather-clad warriors clustered on the foreshore, so we put in carefully. Their chief, a man with plaited black beard and copper-scaled armour, waded to his thighs and shouted questions. Jason mentioned the killing of Amycus, and the tribesmen cheered. We had slain the man who once burned their town and they went mad with joy. Pollux had all the food and black-haired young women he could handle.

So we rested a few days. The black-bearded king told us of the dangers ahead. And here, we heard a name — Medea. Daughter of the king, full of dark witch-power, she was a priestess of the Mother, and I felt fear at this. No matter how far we ventured, always we were meeting the Mother.

And as though her very name changed good luck

to bad, our fortunes changed. Idmon, a good fighter, was hunting boar in the shoreline marshes when a fierce old tusker ripped his stomach out. He died. Tiphys, who was his special friend, went crazy with grief and wandered through the same marshes, to die. So we burned them together and heaped an earth mound over their ashes, their oars stuck as markers.

I felt a foreboding, cold as that skeleton cave on Lemnos. We were two good men less; the first, apart from poor Hylas, who had died on our voyage. I had liked Tiphys; he came from a fishing town too and talked to me more than the others did. Now suddenly there was a shadow on our voyage and, still, the endless unknown shoreline ahead. Anceaus, a wry little Athenian with brown hair and a hook nose, took Tiphys's place at the stern.

We passed another town but did not stop. The people followed a strange religious cult of sex and even coupled in the streets. Their women waded out to their knees, calling to us, but only Zetes wanted to go ashore. He was always lusting and had even wanted to remain behind on Lemnos. Jason said you could not knock sense into his head, even with a corn grinder.

Another town lay ahead. One that gave us a dark vision of the future.

Before it, lay a long stretch of beach with sand as black as the shores of Hades-underworld. The town walls were grimy, the people silent and bad-tempered, clad in filthy leather. They washed particles of iron from their black sands and smelted it into little block-shaped ingots, arrowheads and weapon blades. They did not till soil or pasture flocks. They only smelted out their iron and sold it to passing traders, many traders, from all around these shores.

It was a depressing place. Black smoke hung over their black shore, lit with the red charcoal fires of their forges. They were slow of speech, their eyes red-rimmed in soot-stained faces; everything about them was a grubby black. The streams ran dark, the trees all cut down for charcoal; on their stumps, everywhere, the black ash drifted. The heartbeat of their land was the clang of hammers, pounding their iron into shape.

Our heroes in their bronze armour felt uneasy here. The people ignored us and even their silence mocked. There was no good drinking water so we did not stay. On the way back, I saw an old man struggling with a basket of iron blades. His hair would have been white with age if it were not stained black. I offered to help with the basket but he growled and squinted, shaking his head.

A thought came to me. Jason's gold seal was around my neck. I jerked it off and pointed to his basket. Long and well-shaped dagger blades they were. He grunted, took my gold seal and snuffled over it suspiciously. Then cackled something in his unknown tongue, probably that this young fool had overpaid him, and pushed a blade into my hand. It was heavy, oddly cold, in my hands.

We pushed off and even *Argos* quivered, as though glad to let clean salt air wash away the stench and smoke of that black shore. I went up to Jason on the bow where he stood, one hand on the

98

Athena-prow. I gave him the blade; his sharp eyes noted already that my seal was gone.

He balanced it lightly, passing a finger along the sharp blade. 'Why do you give me this?'

'You saved my life, bringing me on this voyage.' I hesitated, then shrugged. 'And I might not get a chance later on.'

Jason looked at me consideringly. 'You've grown, Pylos.' He didn't just mean I was taller, either. 'What do you think of heroes now?'

'I think you are a great leader,' I replied. 'A great prince.'

'Therefore you respect me?' That little questioning smile. 'What would you say to this?'

'This' was the dagger-point suddenly pricking my armpit. An inch deep and my life was over. Jason was still smiling, tightly. 'If your blood bought success for this voyage, a prince would spill it without thinking twice.'

'Would you, master?' I asked.

His grin became slightly more easy. 'I am still learning about the duties of princehood.' He traced the dagger down the foredeck rail and it left a deep mark in the tough cypress.

'Iron is the master of bronze,' he said at last. 'If those numberless tribes beyond Colchis get iron weapons then our bronze civilisation will fall.' His old smile came back. 'Another good reason for Greeks to make their presence known here.'

Jason the thinker and Jason the dreamer: two men in the same body.

The next day we scrubbed all the sooty filth from *Argos*. Butes, who was skilled in leatherwork, made a handle and scabbard for the dagger. Jason wore it on his belt after that and often his hand closed around it. He was not thinking about me, though. He was thinking about iron.

Now we were being watched. Now the shoreline bulked into high cliffs. Atop them came movement. We glimpsed brown-clad figures on little ponies. Then, from a massive jutting headland, came the gleam of armour and the hiss of arrows. Jason yelled to raise shields and we stood out to sea.

Later legends would say the birds in those cliffs were brazen-metal creatures, who shot their feathers like arrows. But these were real arrows flitting around *Argos*, making Steersman Anceaus skip and yell as they struck the deck around him. The ambushers in those cliffs sprung their trap too soon. On the wind came a distant noise of fighting and we saw the brown-clad horse people again.

Somebody did not want us to reach Colchis. Did someone else protect us?

An island lay ahead. And four young men waded towards us, yelling, shouting they were castaways, their ship wrecked as they came to find us. We met them in full armour and shields but they were alone — and said they were the sons of Prixus, who flew on the golden ram!

Jason kept his face smooth when they said this. We stayed there the night and built our fires. No sign of a wrecked ship anywhere. Good liars these half-Greeks might be but not nearly as clever as Jason.

He served food and wine, appearing to drink cup for cup; but I knew his tricks. Soon their leader, Prontis, was babbling foolishly.

Colchis was less than a week away; the King, Aeetes, old and near death. His daughter, Medea, and his son, Apsyrtus, were children of different mothers — and worshipped different gods. Medea was daughter of the Mother Goddess; Apsyrtus worshipped the wind and storm gods of the great nomad tribes.

And King Aeetes, babbled half-Greek Prontis, wished Medea to marry the Great King of the nomads. Apsyrtus did not — it would make her too powerful. They were sworn enemies and our arrival might tip the scales. All of us, Jason most of all, realized that a dark whirlpool of politics lay ahead. One question Prontis avoided answering. Who left him and his companions on the island? And we did not trust them.

So we took the 'castaways' on board and pulled onward to Colchis, past more high cliffs and dark tangled forest. Behind the cliffs now, mountains stretched far into the sky, with green forest in the lower slopes, then jagged white ridges like axe blades of ice. There, Prontis yelled, the Gods long ago chained Prometheus, for stealing fire and giving it to humans.

A Greek legend-mountain. So, long before, did Greeks come here? I looked up, all of us did, wondering if somewhere on those icy ridges were the massive chains that bound Prometheus for daring to steal from the Gods. Or the giant eagle that ripped his liver each day.

Now we rowed beside marshy river mouths, thick with brown silt that slopped from our oars. On the shores of one, those brown-clad riders reappeared, sitting on their ponies and watching us. The animals put down their heads and drank. Jason would have taken *Argos* closer, but Prontis caught his arm, his voice tense and urgent.

'That is the river of the Amazons! Medea's people, sworn to her.'

'Women warriors?' Zetes spat rudely overboard. 'They look nothing!'

'They are something, as you will discover,' replied Prontis. 'And the trees might hide a thousand more.'

We were not close enough to see the faces of those riders. They sat on their ponies with an insolent grace, watching as we drew away. They carried short bows, no other weapons we could see. But even at this distance, Prontis was pale and fearful.

Another day's rowing. A night we moored in the thick muddy water. A maze of reed clumps closed around us; Prontis stood in the prow, guiding us. Fish-life flickered underwater; once, a huge pale monster, two metres long, passed beside the ship. Another river opened ahead and Prontis signalled us to stop. Then he pointed.

Ahead lay Colchis.

Again, we spent the night on our oars. Prontis said not to approach the city until dawn. Around us, the darkness was heavy with the distant smells of unseen Colchis. Smoke, human bodies, oil. So many hundreds of sea-leagues had we come and now our journey ended.

No Greeks in living history had come so far. There was a man's strength in my arms and back now; my hands were toughened and hard. I rested my head on my crossed arms. I thought suddenly of Ixlos and wondered about my life with her; a father by now, or dead in the death cave? And despite what we had gone through together, I still did not feel part of this crew.

Something else Prontis and his brothers had told us. Yes, Colchis was a golden land and, in the up-country streams, they pinned sheep fleeces into the water. The thick tangled wool caught grains of gold carried down from the mountains. So there were golden fleeces of a sort; one so rich that even the head and horns were gold, and this lay in the Mother shrine tended by Medea.

'And do not think you will ever take it,' he said solemnly. 'It is guarded by a dragon monster that never sleeps.'

Civilized Greeks do not believe the fairy stories of half-barbarians. The heroes had exchanged grins, even Jason put his hand over his mouth. But now, with waking bird sounds around us, in the pale morning light, the stories seemed more real. The thick waters, the buzz of insects, the heavy clumps of rush; a swamp mist, low and thick. An emotion coiled tightly in my stomach. Not quite fear.

Foreboding.

As though in the half-light, evil was gathering. As though all the dangers we had passed already were games for children. The others could feel it too. It was in the way they sat up, listening for a distant sound coming closer. Seeming to gather evil, as thick and close as the mist. A distant tapping noise.

The tapping grew. Jason did not have to rouse the crew. All were listening. Prontis and his brothers had slipped away during the night; a fish-splash overboard, the call of a morning bird and the shrill hum of biting insects. Through the thick reeds and mist, the tapping came louder and we knew what the sound was.

Footsteps.

My sense of foreboding grew stronger. Around me, hands closed on swords. Only demons could walk on a swamp. Now I could hear unknown words, sung in a low throaty voice that shivered me, cold as the mist. A shadowed figure now came towards us, seeming to walk on the brown-black water, stopping now and looking down at our ship.

No swamp demon this, but a woman, standing on a narrow board walkway; still singing and swinging her hips so that her flounced skirts rustled like the reeds themselves. A short cloak fell to her waist. She was in shadow, black hair in snaky tangled ringlets around her dark face. She stepped down onto the foredeck of *Argos* as though she owned it; uttered three words in the same throaty voice.

'I am Medea.'

Chapter 11

A lot made sense now. Including those three 'cast-aways' on the island. Medea — like all Colchis — knew we were coming. Doubtless the news was brought by those fleet brown riders we saw on the clifftops. And she had decided not to wait for us to reach her golden city.

Now she looked up and down the rowing benches as though she knew us all. Her gaze lingered on Jason. And all of us looked at her. Witch woman, priestess-daughter of Rhea-Mother.

She was short and slim-waisted, her low-cut pink blouse drawn in tightly, her flounced skirt in layers of red and blue linen, her short cape of fine doeskin, stiff with thick gold stitching like twining snakes. Heavy gold bracelets circled each wrist and long gold pendants hung from each ear. A multi-layered gold necklace lay around her throat, each link shaped as a laurel leaf. A gold headband patterned like a snake was almost hidden by her black curly hair. In the centre of her forehead, held in place by a fine black cord, a third golden eye flashed, even in the mist.

'Have you finished inspecting me, Greeks of Icolos?' she asked.

'Sparta,' said Castor and Pollux together.

'Athens,' said Anceaus. And, of course, all the others had to say their own states. Mitlos, Skyros, Mycenae, Tiryns, Corinth, Athens. Medea listened in silence, her brown face expressionless; a strong face, her brown eyes like fine pottery catching the sunlight. There was power and royal pride in her bearing, and something else. She fascinated but made you afraid. All our heroes sensed that except Zetes, who was drooling open-mouthed at her. His brother punched him hard, twice.

'Lady, is it proper for you to meet us alone?' asked Jason.

Medea just smiled. Those dark eyes examined Jason as he came slowly up the walkway, then she gestured, her gold bracelets clinking. In the distance, through the thinning mist, was the twinkle of spearpoints. Iron spearpoints. Of course Medea had not come alone.

'You are welcome on *Argos*,' said Jason.

Medea kept smiling. Her lips were gold-painted too, her voice low and full of power. 'But Jason, is *Argos* welcome in Colchis?'

'Perhaps you can tell us, lady.' He smiled too.

None of us moved. Not because of those iron spearheads in the distance; a closer unseen prickle. We sensed that around us in the long reeds were sharp iron-tipped arrows on bows at full stretch; her brown riders, now dismounted and up to their waists in water. Medea had gold rings on each finger, set with red jewels like the eye of a snake. A single twitch of those gold-ringed fingers and our lives would end. Jason just smiled and waited for her answer.

'Perhaps I can,' she said at last.

Already there was something between them. Jason the voyager, with only his wits. Medea the princess, with her gold-lidded eyes and gold mouth. Now she turned with a swirl of those heavy skirts and stepped back onto the walkway, her thick-heeled shoes tapping as she went. A gold-ringed finger beckoned Jason to follow.

He did, his leather sandals making less sound. We learned later there were many such walkways criss-crossing the marsh for hunting and food gathering. They walked a little way in and talked in low tones. We sat motionless, all too aware of those unseen arrows. Medea stepped close to Jason; her bracelets clinked as she put a hand on his shoulder. Standing tiptoe in her thick-soled red shoes, she whispered in his ear.

A long moment she whispered and her bracelets jangled again. Then she left. The faint jingle of her jewellery and the tap-tap of her footsteps died away in the mist. Around us, the green reeds seemed to bristle less, as though that unseen menace withdrew also.

There was danger in this. Beside me, Butes pressed his teeth against his lower lip. There was uncertain shifting as Jason returned. Royal princesses do not appear on swamp walkways to meet unwelcome strangers. But Jason jumped back on the foredeck, his mouth shut, thinking hard. He signalled steering and oars and *Argos* backed with a sudden loud splash that made me jump. Around us in the swamp was no sign of life. Jason spoke, his words uncertain; as though they were Medea's not his.

'The way to Colchis is open,' he said. 'We are welcome.'

He did not speak loudly — as though that were wrong in this haunted misty place. Our oars slapped in the sluggish muddy water, out of the thick reeds and into a broader riverway. In front of us now, across the reeds, came the noise of a waking city. At least all that sounded normal. The mist disappeared, the blue sky of morning overhead. And Jason told us of his conversation with Medea.

There was feuding between Medea and her brother, Prince Apsyrtus. And King Aeetes distrusted the coming of Greeks because our arrival might tip an uneasy power balance. Medea, he said, would assure the king that we were peaceful traders (of course he would believe that of a shipload of warriors!) but Jason said we should tread carefully. Beside me, as we strained on the oars, Butes muttered he would rather tread through a pit of vipers.

And so we approached Colchis, the golden city.

The town was behind a high palisade of massive sharp-pointed logs that must have needed as much skill to raise as our stone-built walls. A wooden jetty ran underneath them, jutting out at intervals into piers, all black with age but looking solid. Colchis galleys, low and narrow-gutted, designed for rivers, not the open seas, were moored in rows. King Aeetes had a big navy but all the ships were empty; their oars stacked, their masts unstepped and laid neatly down the middle. The jetty and wall were centred with a huge double gate, flanked with heavy wooden pillars.

As we came alongside, the gates began to open.

'Hands clear of weapons,' said Jason quietly. 'Medea assures us of a good welcome.'

Out tramped a column of guards, short men in high leather caps and leather jackets covered with horn plates — primitive armour but good — and there were many of them. They wore cross-strapped leggings and carried two javelins each. A hundred of them, tramping quick-step, filled the jetty in moments.

Now, out of the gateway, rode a man on a stocky pony. He wore bronze-scaled armour, each scale set with a hawk of gold; on his head, a pointed gold helmet, horsehair crest fluttering in the breeze. A long gold-hilted sword across his gold-mounted saddle; gold-studded reins too, I noticed. He paused between his silent rows of spearmen. He and his men grim and silent.

'A good welcome?' Butes muttered beside me. 'I should hate to see a bad one.'

'You should not have come, Greek pirates!' Prince Apsyrtus, his brown face set like Medea's, his voice high-pitched; exactly the same tone of ruthless power. 'Here is your welcome to Colchis.'

His men swung up their light spears, ready to cast. Ours were already grabbing for shield and sword. Apsyrtus inflated his lungs to shout the order over our desperate unready clatter. And more death, a line of archers appeared on the wooden battlements of the city. If the spears did not skewer us, their arrows would feather *Argos* like a ghastly bird of death.

Nothing happened. Apsyrtus was staring up at the battlements, his mouth open. Beside me, Jason suddenly chuckled — because the archers had their bows trained on the spearmen.

Now as I looked more closely, I could see long black hair below the pointed leather caps; every face beardless and smooth-cheeked, blue vertical scars on their high cheekbones, a third blue eye tattooed in the forehead.

Medea's Amazon warriors.

Now she appeared herself, between them, hands on hips. First she looked directly at her brother. Nothing was said, the third gold eye flashed. Apsyrtus exhaled with a long gusty sigh and sheathed his sword. Those Amazon bows were more powerful than they looked and, at that range, would penetrate armour and body. Apsyrtus scowled again — at us — and swung his pony around. His men tramped back quickly into the wooden town. Medea waited till the last was gone, then smiled down broadly.

'Welcome to Colchis, Jason. The king awaits you, so please do not sit there all day.'

Medea had timed her arrival to the very last moment. Of course she intended to. Not to scare us further; more to humiliate her brother. Now she came down onto the jetty and walked up, her gold clinking.

'No weapons and no armour,' she said.

'My lady,' replied Jason and bowed.

She smiled but watched sharply as we got ready. Each man put on his best tunic, crumpled and stained though they were from the long voyage. Even our daggers we left behind, forming up on the jetty under Jason. Two warriors were left behind as ship guards; the others and I followed him through the open gates. The silent ranks of those brown-clad Amazons closed the gates — then closed around us. Each bore a short sword and spear; shield and bow slung across their backs.

Medea led the way with Jason, her hips swinging, her gold clinking and her wooden shoe heels tapping …

Up into the silent streets of Colchis, the 'golden' city.

Chapter 12

Ahead, the tramp of soldiers had died away. For a moment, the silence reminded me of Lemnos. Only a moment, because Colchis was like no sunlit Greek city of flat-roofed white plaster houses and stone. It was a city of wood.

All of it was wood; the narrow streets made of squared and levelled logs, laid endwise; the tall narrow houses with slanting roofs of thick-sawn timber. The doors were closed, the narrow windows tightly shuttered. No smoke rose from the fireholes in the roofs. No sound of life, save our own footsteps and our Amazon escort. They marched quickly in their sleeveless leather tunics and leggings, not looking at us once.

Further into the city we went. More narrow streets, and every door was closed, their overhead lintels seeming to frown, as though Colchis were a sullen wooden beast, resenting our intrusion; the city pressing around us in thick silence. I hoped Medea had the power that she said she did. She walked in front, her thick-soled shoes tapping, her gold jingling. Jason walked beside her, glancing at the silent doorways.

'Colchis does not seem to like us,' he said.

'You will see if you are liked, soon enough,' she returned, with a sideways look and a swagger of her hips.

'We can teach you to build in stone,' he said, thinking already to civilize them like Greeks.

111

Another of her sideways gold-lidded looks. 'Not everyone wants to build in stone, Jason.'

Meaning, keep his civilizing remarks to himself for now. Jason took the hint and fell silent again. Before us now was a large square of wooden blocks, like paving stones, laid in the spiral pattern like a circling snake. Across the square were the timber pillars of a palace.

It had a touch of Greek style, but there was nothing Greek in the way it shone and dazzled. Gold plastered the pillars, thick as paste on an old woman's cheeks; on the big double doors were two circling servants, the hawk sign above them. And over that, the big curling ram's horns that were the totem of King Aeetes.

Spearmen in high bronze helmets stood at the door, their long oxhide shields before them; the king's guard this time, and Medea's Amazon escort fell back. She walked on through the opening palace gates and the crew of the *Argos* followed. I tried to keep my face like theirs — closed, unafraid, showing Greek pride. And I was proud to be in their company, even in my battered leather tunic. Each man wore his best cloak, linen kilt and high-strapped sandals — civilized fashion; only barbarians covered their legs in trousers. We had a lot to teach these people.

A dark foyer now, smelling old and dusty. More guards, archers with flat noses, round shields and face tattoos in blue spirals. A second set of doors opened, the noise seeming choked in this thick dark silence. Medea stepped ahead of us, tripping quickly across the long room to the end — the throne room.

She dropped a low, dancing curtsey to the man seated there. King Aeetes.

And oh, he was old! Dressed in a full-length wool robe that crackled with age like him. It was sewn with a mixing pattern of hawk wings and gold spirals; more of those red serpent-eye jewels. On his head, a ram's-horn helmet, with eagle-feather crest, of pure gold. Even I could see the forces of two different faiths, of the earth and of the sky. Their balance lay in his person.

And he was old.

Under the ram's-horn helmet, white cobweb wisps of hair descended over cheeks the colour of old dried bark; a big nose and thin bloodless lips. His eyes shone with that brown-pottery life like Medea's, watching us as we walked across his big wooden hall, dark with years of smoke, past the big centre hearth. The carving and any inlaid colours on the wall patterns were long since crusted and darkened. Even his throne was dark. Medea had glided up beside him and now looked back at us.

'On your knees before the Great King.'

Jason hesitated a moment, then fell to his knees. The others did too, although Castor and Pollux — being Spartans — were last and scowled. The floorboards were thick wood, ridged and chipped, covered with dirt, bone fragments and dry straw. There was silence. Around the throne was a crowd of Colchis nobles, bearded men wrapped in long cloaks. All of us waiting for the king to speak.

King Aeetes looked at us with no expression at all. Prince Apsyrtus, now bare-headed, was on his other side. The king's throne had thick armrests, long and curving. His wrinkled old hands, skinny as dried bird claws, tapped them now. His voice was crackly too, and he glanced at Apsyrtus before speaking.

'My son, I thought you were welcoming the Greeks.'

Medea interposed smoothly. 'My little brother kindly left the arrangements with me.'

King Aeetes cackled. His look darted from one to another, quick as a hawk. Apsyrtus frowned sulkily and Aeetes just cackled again. Then he turned his brown eyes on us and we saw the strong force in them. In the silence even the slight scratch of one long fingernail on the armrest of his throne could be heard. His voice came again, like the creak of old dried leather.

'Jason, what is my throne made of?' he asked.

Jason made to rise but glimpsed the warning flicker in Medea's eyes. 'Elephant ivory,' he replied, still on his knees.

'Trust a Greek to know treasure.' Aeetes' laugh sounded like the crow of a very elderly rooster. 'What else about it?'

'The tusks are longer than any I have seen,' said Jason.

Aeetes tittered again. We all knelt silent, our heads up. Whatever happened, we were Greeks and did not frighten easily. Aeetes leaned back, tapping his fingers on the curved armrests. 'From no living elephant,' he replied. 'These once lived on the frozen wastelands beyond the grass ocean. Only their tusks and bones remain now. Why am I telling you this, Jason?'

'To show your kingdom stretches to the outer limits of the world, Great King.'

'A flattering answer,' said Aeetes, softly.

'The answer you wanted, Great King,' said Jason.

His easy grin came as he spoke. I was watching Aeetes. I saw a flash of wrinkled anger, then something else. Respect. He wasn't used to simple bold answers — or how shrewdly Jason slipped through his guard. He cackled again but his next words had a slightly cold edge to them.

'So you come for our Golden Fleece, eh?'

'If so, we are not the first,' said Jason.

'No. You are not.' Now the words were very cold and Aeetes shook his head slowly. 'Heroes from lands you have never heard of. And those you have. Colchis attracts all, Jason. Why, once even a refugee Greek princeling, on the overland trails. What happened to him, my daughter?'

'He died here, father. Thinking he could teach us Greek ways.' Her brown face as expressionless as in the swamp — was it only this morning? 'Those who come here do not always leave.'

'Sometimes we send their heads back,' snarled Apsyrtus.

Jason ignored them both. 'Great King, we come for trade,' he said.

King Aeetes just smiled and turned to his son. His voice now like a knife sawing rope. 'Apsyrtus, what shall we do with them?

'Kill them.'

A murmur of assent came from some of the cloak-wrapped councillors. Among them I saw Prontis and his companions, unmoving, their faces pale with fear. 'Fifty Greeks today means a thousand tomorrow. And the end of Colchis.'

King Aeetes cackled delightedly as though the answer pleased him. His sharp brown eyes turned to Medea. I know she was as much in his power as we were. But she shrugged, with one of her throaty chuckles. 'Father, they are Greek pirates, hungry for gold. And you will do as you please.'

Aeetes cackled again, flapping one thin hand like a scrap of threadbare sailcloth. On both sides, his guards stood poised with their deadly spears. His brown eyes shone with cruel power; those bloodless lips moved, about to speak.

I don't know what Jason said to Medea on the walkway. But not even she controlled her father, so the challenge lay with Jason. As it did when the Trojan galley ran us down. When he took the helm at the Clashing Rocks. Now, with death looming, all our lives in the balance, he did the same. Risking the spears, he rose. He stood facing Aeetes.

'I may be all those things, Great King.' His big loose grin again and he actually dusted the dirt of the palace floor from his kilt before going on. 'But I have been on my knees long enough. I will hear your decision standing.'

I think that was all the advice Medea gave him. Be bold. And now, beside me, Butes stood. Zetes, Castor, Pollux, me scrambling up too. An amazed stir went through the dark hall. All sound went as though every man was holding his breath.

Aeetes glared. His old hand twitched. His lips moved again, showing yellowed old teeth. Then something else happened. From somewhere overhead came the high scream of a hunting eagle, repeated twice. It sounded clear in the thick gloom, like the sharp sound of ripping cloth.

Aeetes looked up. The gold eagle crest of his helmet flashed. Only later did we find out that Aeetes was very superstitious about eagles. And certainly the cry, from somewhere overhead, was very well timed. And when that cry came, all the court looked up — except Medea. Aeetes slumped back into his chair, coughing and gulping. Medea patted him tenderly on the back.

'Father,' she said, as though just remembering, 'are not Greeks supposed to be very crafty? Perhaps this one is crafty enough to pass a little test?'

Aeetes coughed again and his golden crown tilted sideways. Medea pushed it gently back into place and smiled sweetly at her brother. Apsyrtus was white with rage, glaring, about to speak. But Aeetes flapped his hand for silence and the strength came back to his voice. His brown eyes shone again.

'Yes, a little test. Is that not fair, Jason?'

'Yes, Great King.' What else could Jason say? 'And what is the test?'

'Oh, you'll find out soon. It will amuse you, I'm sure.'

And he laughed in that spiteful cackly way, his thin shoulders shaking. And, surprisingly, so did Apsyrtus, with unpleasant scorn. Medea was chuckling, all the councillors laughing; even the grim-faced spearmen broke into smiles. All the great hall rang with noise and we stood silent, because there was little humour in that laughter.

Soon, very soon, we would see the joke.

Chapter 13

Aeetes dismissed us, after that. His guardsmen took us outside to where the Amazons still waited. Still in silence, we were taken to a long hall by the palace. The wooden walls were smoothed with clay and painted with huge humped two-horned bulls, fearsome like everything here; wild forest ox, from the dark northern lands.

The doors stayed open and a group of Amazons with spears — and their ever-present little bows — stood outside. Palace slavewomen, who averted their eyes from us, brought in bedding and food; bread, cattle-meat and little wooden pails of milk. Zetes tasted some and spat sharply.

'Mare's milk!' he said.

'Drink it!' said Jason sharply.

He sat apart from us, with a piece of flat bread and a cup of the sour-tasting milk. It was somehow fermented and made us feel more lighthearted. We sat against the walls, eating a little. Zetes now took a taste for the milk and downed cup after cup.

The Amazons stood in the doorway, eyeing us without speaking. I caught the eye of a younger one and she frowned back at me. Zetes hiccupped and nudged me.

'Careful there, boy. Some wild women like only one part of a man to eat.'

Foolishly I asked, 'Which part?' So Zetes hooked his arm around my shoulder and told me exactly which part, in a whisper loud enough for all Colchis to hear. Then he slapped my back, hard.

'Don't worry, lad. You'd only make a snack!'

Everyone chuckled and even Jason smiled. To make things worse, I think the Amazons understood too. Trust Medea to select guards who understood Greek. Anyway, the next time I looked at the young Amazon, she ran her tongue over her lips — with a quick vixen flash of her teeth.

Castor drained his cup too. 'I wonder what sort of test Aeetes had in mind,' he said. 'Others have tried to take the Fleece ...'

Butes shrugged. He was tired, like all of us, after a broken night's sleep. 'Maybe whether we can still walk and talk after his guards have put their spears into us.' For once he was not joking.

More Amazons arrived outside. A sharp order, and six bustled quickly in — and grabbed me! Jason shouted but they hauled me out, kicking the door shut. They made no sound but hauled me down a dark wooden corridor. One of them was the young woman who overheard Zetes, and horrible visions flashed through my mind. She glanced sideways at me with a quick malicious grin.

Up a flight of stairs they dragged me, my toes stubbing painfully on the wooden steps; another corridor, another flight of steps, I think connecting to the palace. At a landing now, hung with smoke-stained drapes. I just had time to notice the snake patterns embroidered on them as the door opened and I was kicked inside. I rolled head over heels on a big sheepskin rug.

The room was many-sided, nearly circular; a narrow

window covered with scraped fish skin let in some light. I saw more long wall drapes, stained by the smoking oil lamps set in bronze brackets. Pale fish-light and flickering lamplight chased snaky shadows everywhere, but there was enough light for me to see the grim dark look on Medea's tight-lipped face.

She was standing beside a small stool, made of that dark yellow ivory with golden claws on each of the three legs. She still wore her flounced skirt and doeskin cape, black hair tumbling loose on her doe-skin shoulders, her brown eyes like those of a hunt-ing hawk. Already it seemed years ago, not this morning, that she came to our ship from the misty swamplands.

'What colour is Greek blood?' she asked.

I just gaped. I could not think of anything to say. That splendid ivory stool, chased my foolish thoughts, why is she not sitting on it? An Amazon spear butt jabbed into my back and I swallowed, forcing myself to think properly.

'Red,' I gasped, sensing bad black danger in the flickering shadows.

Medea just shrugged. 'Greeks are such liars,' she said.

She looked over my head as though I did not exist. Her guards held me down and that throaty voice crawled on my skin like the touch of evil.

'Jason says he came only for trade. But he desires our most sacred possession. No, we can believe nothing a Greek says, even to the colour of his blood.'

The guards held me tight. I opened my mouth and a spear butt thumped again. Shut up. Medea poked her feet out from under the hem of her skirt, pushing one red shoe against the other. She still looked over my head and spoke the next words almost to herself.

'We shall see if he lies. Cut off his head.'

Behind, came the low deadly swish of a sword whipped from its scabbard. An Amazon — that young one — stepped in front of me. Two guards pressed their spear butts into my shoulders to keep me kneeling. The young woman raised her sword, her eyes gleaming.

I saw a beheading at Icolos. A crazy man who flung manure around the shrine of Apollo. A messy butchering because he screamed and struggled. I shut my eyes, tried to remember I was Greek and proud. But the fear must have shown in my face. My throat tickled and I had to swallow, open my eyes. The shadow of the Amazon sword still on the floor. Then somebody chuckled. A shrill rooster sound, followed by crackly words.

'A finger perhaps, Medea. He will need his head for talking.'

King Aeetes was there. One of the drapes pulled back to disclose another entrance. His guards filed in after him. He took his place on the stool — no wonder Medea had not sat there. Prince Apsyrtus was beside him, still sullen. And I realized, like a slow-witted peasant, that all this was done to scare me. Aeetes had timed his entrance well.

'Any of the crew will know more than this boy,' growled Apsyrtus. 'When you want to know what happens in the barn, ask the bull not the rat.'

Aeetes gave his thin titter. 'No, my son, ask the rat. He scuttles everywhere.'

Then he stared at the Amazon who still had her sword out. She stepped back, dropping it on the floor with a clatter. Aeetes turned his wide eyes to Medea who bowed her head in apology — and even looked scared. She should have ordered that the sword be sheathed as soon as he was in the room. Aeetes pressed his hand to his forehead to recollect his thoughts. He looked at me.

'Boys hear things, eh? Warriors talk in front of servants because they do not matter.'

'Great King, I know very little,' I replied.

I tried frantically to think what Jason would have said. Oh, for a moment of his wit! Beside the king, Medea blinked her brown eyes at me, the third gold wisdom-eye flashing above. She did it slowly, with deliberation. A warning?

'Then tell us what you know,' she said. 'Do not lie, because you know the test for that already.'

And a slight stress on the know. Her hand on her gold leaf-layered necklace, forefinger pressing to her pink blouse. You know nothing of me, said those gestures. Aeetes stared at me, his brown eyes wide as an owl's. So I began talking. Perhaps truth could save me.

The building of *Argos*, King Pelias and the wooden pegs (Aeetes tittering in approval of such a kingly trick) and the gathering of our hero crew; Lemnos and the skeleton-cave (Medea's little approving nod, a glance at her brother); then our voyage; Heracles, Phineus and the Clashing Rocks, the long long coastal row to Colchis.

While I spoke, the lamps guttered, casting their flickering shadows. An hour passed, I think. Medea stood beside her father, a hand lightly on his shoulder. Aeetes' sharp brown eyes, in his dark wrinkled face, never left mine.

Finally, our arrival in Colchis. Medea's gold-ringed finger flashed again, as though in warning. So I did not mention her coming onto *Argos*. Only that we reached Colchis this morning.

Aeetes was silent a long time. One of the lamps was guttering badly and Medea reached a graceful hand to snuff the wick. The room grew a little darker. It was already hot, smelling of bodies and mutton-fat, and my own fear. Then Aeetes stirred himself and drew four little yellow-ivory balls from a pouch on his belt. He began to toss them, one skinny hand to the other.

'What am I doing?' he asked.

'Juggling, Great King,' I answered.

'A king learns to keep several balls in the air at the same time.' The balls juggled faster so they blurred. 'Your Pelias juggled Jason out of his kingdom, a clever king, that.' Then, sharply, 'But you don't trust Jason. Why should I?'

I let the hesitation show on my face; it was all the answer he needed. And he was right. I told him all about how cunning Jason was — and how brave. But not if he was honest.

'He's a prince —' I stopped. King Aeetes leaned forward like an old snake. Then the right words came on my tongue as though placed there. 'Princes don't think like ordinary people.'

Aeetes gave his high thin cackle. One ivory ball flew high into the air. Apsyrtus glowered again and Medea's face remained smooth. The Great King coughed and dropped his little balls back into the pouch. His shoulders drooped in the gold-sewn robe and his gold crown seemed very heavy.

'No, we do not. We have to juggle too many balls in the air for that! And if we drop the balls, someone might take them. Might they not, my children?' They knew better than to answer.

I was still trapped and scared. No more than a bug to be crushed by these people. But I remembered what Jason had said. 'Great King, juggle your balls behind stone walls. Greeks will build them for you.'

Aeetes shook his head, suddenly looking tired. 'Boy, the horse tribes of the grass oceans are numberless. Grow the wings of an eagle and fly over them a hundred days, you would still not reach the end of their host. They would come over the highest wall like waves over sand.'

I was puzzled and forgot my fear a moment. 'Then why don't they?'

King Aeetes pointed a skinny brown finger at me. 'Answer that with your Greek wits and I will let you live.'

Silence came again, apart from the King's wheezy breathing. The flat burned smell of mutton fat became stronger and the shadows darker. Outside, the sun was setting and the fish skin window glowed pale red like a single glaring eye.

It was the most important thing I ever had to think about. But somehow the answer came more easily than I thought. Perhaps because I had been thinking about it — and yes, I do have Greek wits — about what Heracles said, even how Medea's gold forehead eye flashed as she welcomed us to the unknown land. So my words came, slowly, in the utter silence.

'Great King, we all thought this voyage was to the end of the world. But this is not the end. Just the beginning of another. The horse tribes have no use for our world. But they will not let us touch theirs.' Now I dared something because, after death, they could not hurt me. 'Are those the balls you juggled, Great King?'

The silence went on until it hurt. Aeetes looked at me, his eyes like brown stone. Then abruptly he slapped the little pouch and, inside, the balls clanked. He stood up and left, with a swirl of his gold-embroidered cloak. The spearmen followed; Prince Apsyrtus too, and quickly, not wishing to be left alone with his sister's guards.

Now a change came over Medea's face, so frightening that I thought it was death anyway. She went a chalky white under her brown skin and her eyes shone with fury in that dark room. She walked over, stalking in a stiff-legged way and held out her hand.

Not to me, to the Amazon who kept her sword out when the Great King entered. Medea spat words in her own language, touched with snake venom, it seemed. The young woman paled and quickly bent to hand her the sword.

None of the others moved. Holding the sword out in both hands, Medea turned her head and looked at me. She spoke strangely, her brown eyes burning with that cold fire. 'Tell Jason, the test is very simple. He must plough a field and sow seed. Surely a Greek prince can do that, eh?'

I was safe from death and risked one question.

Maybe not foolishly because, even though Medea looked so angry, among princes and princesses, play-acting and reality changed places at will.

'Would you have cut my head off?'

And straightaway I knew how much peril I was still in. Not because of her anger but from the sudden little smile on her gold-painted lips. And her voice, composed again, throaty and cold.

'I may yet. Now excuse me, I must give a lesson in manners.'

Two of the Amazons pulled me out and the door slammed behind. As I was dragged down the stairs, I heard Medea speak again, her words unknown again, her tone sharp and merciless. Then a cry, cut short. I never knew what Medea's lesson in manners was and I did not see the guardswoman again.

Chapter 14

Back in the chamber, Jason made me repeat everything that went on, several times over — even about
the Amazon and her sword. King Aeetes was old and
feared assassination; more than ever, Medea must
show herself the dutiful loving daughter. And Jason
frowned over the test.

'Plough a field ...?' He shook his head, it was too
simple. There had to be a hidden meaning somewhere.

Zetes and Butes poked me, asking if anything was
missing after my encounter with the Amazons. Had
I looked? asked Butes grinning. Would I notice?
asked Zetes slyly, and all the crew roared with heart-
less laughter. I think they were glad to see me
though. I did not know if Jason thought I had handled myself well. But next day, when summoned, he
was told he might bring ten companions. And he
chose me as one — yes, over heroes and warriors.
Yes, and I was proud.

There were some sniffs and growls from the heroes; Jason selecting the ship's boy over them?
Even though I was no longer a boy and had done
just as much. Butes, not chosen, growled unkindly
that I might really come back with something missing, this time. And, he said, I would not have to look
for it — just feel on my neck where my head used
to be.

I replied that Medea and I had already discussed

that. The look of bewilderment on his face was worth seeing.

We were mounted on those stocky little Colchis ponies and rode through the back gate of the city. The front walls that faced the sea were tall, thick and strong, these back walls only an earthen bank with a palisade on top. Perhaps because the only enemy to come from this direction, Jason said, would be the horse tribes. And nothing could stop them.

King Aeetes rode ahead, with Medea. His spearmen were clumped thickly on either side, then came Colchis nobles and more spearmen, clumped around us. Our road curved around a broad expanse of meadow and a wide estuary. Prontis rode beside us and pointed to the estuary. Already there were ships upon it, in the distance.

'The merchants arrive,' he said. 'Soon you will see a market like no other in the world.'

Prince Apsyrtus rode ahead and he looked back. 'Are you sure about that, half-Greek mongrel?' he snarled. He had the nose and eyes of his father but the mean twist to his lips and his weak chin were all his own. 'They have not passed the test yet.'

He smirked, turning his pony, shouldering Prontis roughly away. He grinned at Jason. 'But of course there will be no trouble, eh?' His voice was pitched loud for his own guards and attendants. 'Greeks are master sailors and stone builders. So surely Jason can turn his hand to a little ploughing. His peasant ship's boy will give him lessons.'

His men laughed and he rode on ahead. Prontis kept away from us after that. We knew the test was more than simple ploughing, but nothing else. Even so, Jason rode easily, as though he had no concerns. As though all our lives did not depend on him.

The trail led through foothills and stretches of grassland. I thought of Greece and her rocky coastlines, her bleak brown mountains. Now vast stretches of grassland lay ahead. The sky was dazzling blue and the grass set with tiny yellow flowers; the wind stirred them as though brushing over wavetops. A chill wind blew, perhaps all the way from those frozen icelands where the tusk ivory came from. Jason looked up at the sky, around at the grasslands, seeming not to feel the cold wind.

'Hey, Prontis,' he called across, 'is this the grass ocean?'

Prontis, still pale, shook his head. 'Like a puddle of rainwater to a — great sea,' he answered, then pointed. 'We are here.'

The ploughing paddock was picketed off with sharp oak stakes. A large crowd of Colchis people had already gathered and more were coming. They were tall, the men in their long dark cloaks and high fur or sheepskin hats; the women in brighter colours, faces and heads covered with shawls so that only their eyes could be seen. The men had strong proud faces with long moustaches and curly beards. None, that I could see, carried weapons.

We dismounted. Ahead of us, so did Apsyrtus and he looked over again. 'Hey, Jason, be kind to these worn-out old creatures. They cannot take any rough treatment.'

The cruel pleasure in his words was as cold as the wind. And as he spoke, a loud bellow split the air.

Our ponies fidgeted, the crowd parted and we saw the 'worn-out' creatures. We looked at them, the end of our hopes. They were large, solid and horrible. The black truth behind the king's teasing words.

They were both very big. That was the first thing I saw. Cretan bulls are twenty handspans long but these were even longer. They were thickset and massive, the head growing out of broad shoulders. Heavy muscles bulged and rippled under their gleaming black hides. They dug their forelegs into the earth and rolled their wicked little red eyes. They did not bellow again but gave strangled little noises as though keeping all their fury inside. Their horns were curved and sharp, longer than any I have seen.

I had seen cattle like this before. Painted just as black and awesome on the plastered walls of our guest chambers. The monster wild ox of the northern forests. Their horns had been gilded and flashed sharp as golden pitchforks. In Greece, we gild the horns of sacrificial animals to please the Gods. Here, I think Jason was the sacrifice.

He took off his tunic. His muscles glistened in the sun because he had oiled himself. He wore only a short leather kilt and his cross-strapped leather sandals. The king's spearmen formed a line, silent behind their long hide shields. Now I saw Medea, walking up with King Aeetes. She wore a long red cloak with twining gold-stitched serpents and led a pony in a gold-studded harness. Beside her, Aeetes was wrapped in heavy sheepskin, his thin face glaring sharper than the wind. He croaked, maliciously.

'Now, Jason.' A thin brown hand came out of the

cloak and pointed to the bulls. 'Let us see if we can make a farmer out of you.'

The big crowd laughed. Everyone laughs when a king makes a joke. Apsyrtus grinned but Medea seemed lost in thought; she leaned against her pony, pulling the long braided mane between her fingers. Jason just smiled, that loose daring grin we all knew. He raised a hand to King Aeetes and vaulted lightly over the oak stakes.

'Ready, Great King!' he shouted.

The bulls were already harnessed in thick red bronze-studded leather and he circled around to where the reins lay on the ground. A big pile of fresh droppings steamed like hot pudding. Both the bulls stood quietly but their ears pricked back; their tails began to lightly swish. Beside me was Telamon, who had spent some years in Crete and knew about bulls.

'They seem well-behaved,' I whispered. 'Is that ear-flattening a good sign?'

'No,' he whispered simply back and pulled at his beard. 'This is the strangest ploughing field I have ever seen.

I knew what he meant. The field was of flattened fresh earth, not turf, and broad thick ridges of earth, a knee's length high, some ten of them, ran the length of the field; each was widely spaced from the next. Now Aeetes threw a leather bag to Jason, who opened it. There were polished square chunks of the dark yellow ivory inside.

'Dragon teeth, Jason,' called the King. 'They are magic and will sprout as armed men. Sow me a crop of warriors.'

Jason tucked the bag into his belt and took up the reins. He looped them around his body, grasped the brown wooden handles of the plough and set its bronze blade in the black Colchis earth. His face was expressionless as he shook the reins.

It was like shaking the sound and fury out of each bull.

They bellowed again. They charged forward, their harness taut. Jason straightaway dug in his heels and they ploughed a twin furrow behind the blade. Even if the blade skipped, his heels scored deep marks; he skidded, pulled the length of the field, over the fresh mound of droppings. He fell, hanging by one hand to the plough. We of *Argos* groaned. Was it over already? Prince Apsyrtus laughed; Medea turned her face away. And it would have been the end, for anyone else but Jason.

The bulls paused, as though wondering if they were free of their burden. And Jason bounded up, pulling the reins to turn them into the next furrow. They did anyway — at least half-trained — and swung around with Jason flying behind them, thundering down between those long mounds. So far, he had not sown any dragon's teeth.

This was death for us all. Nobody was meant to win this test. I glanced at King Aeetes, a grim lean figure in his shaggy cloak, his face sharp and frozen in the cold wind. Then beside me, Telamon, whistling and breathing … 'Oh, bravely done!'

The bulls had turned again. But this time — smeared with mud and manure from head to toe — Jason checked them a moment.

Just a moment!

The bulls pulled again, jerked; suddenly I realized what he was doing. Not trying to pull them back, but check and guide as he would the steering oar of *Argos*. This time he kept his balance — and his plough dug a zig-zag line in the earth! We of *Argos* cheered. He was steering them!

The bulls strained as they reached the next line and turned. Their black hides glistened with sweat and their strangled bellows filled the air. They pulled, but Jason pulled back now, his muscles straining. Now came claps and shouts from the Colchis crowd. Medea was looking now and, best of all, the smile was gone from Apsyrtus's face.

They had reached the end of the third furrow. The bulls had slowed and Jason's ploughline became straighter. Now, even as they turned, he grabbed a handful of the ivory chunks — the 'dragon's teeth.' He scattered them in his furrows. The crowd cheered but King Aeetes stood unmoving.

And Jason ploughed!

It was said later that Medea drugged the bulls to take out some of their fire. Perhaps that was true. Perhaps it was one of the secrets she whispered to him in the marshes. But a lesser man would still have been trampled into red mush.

The bulls tried again at the next furrow, fighting each other as much as him. But he took them around, as if he were steering *Argos* free of a tidal rip, with a muscle-wrenching effort, scattering more ivory teeth. But there was something strange about those raised mounds he ploughed between. One of them was sideways trodden by a bull's hoof and moved.

Jason was at the end of the next furrow. He scattered the last of the dragon's teeth and I could see other mounds moving. Apsyrtus put a silver whistle to his lips and blew a sharp pip-pipping whistle. A signal! From the furrows sprang one of his guardsmen. Then another, the loose earth dusting from them. Another, then another; all the ridges breaking apart as Apsyrtus's soldiers sprang from the raised earth. Yes, Jason had raised a crop of armed men and the crowded cheered, thinking it was play-acting.

I knew the truth, though; so did every man of *Argos*. Yes, all of these warriors had sprung to life; in the confusion, a spear would slide gently into Jason's ribs. He was hemmed in by the mob on three sides, the guardsmen between him and our end. Apsyrtus twisted his mean mouth back into a grin. Medea stood, one hand tightly knotted into the pony's mane. Aeetes did not move.

None of them understood what a hero Jason was! Yes, chosen by the Gods, because he bounced back, intent, unconquerable.

He was stinking of earth and manure, stunned and breathless. And soon he would be dead. That was what Colchis thought, judging him by their standards. His own, though, were different, and higher. Now, he proved it. Twenty warriors were coming out of the earth towards him — but they were no match for Jason.

He slipped the reins from his body and let go the plough. He had a dragon's tooth in each hand and jabbed sharply into the bulls' hindquarters. There was nothing strangled about the bellow that split the blue sky now as the bulls bolted — forward!

The warriors saw them coming, but too late. One man went right over the horns, his stomach torn and guts uncoiling like a giant red worm. Another was smashed underneath the sharp hooves. The others scattered, shields clattering, spears cast aside. The bulls smashed into them, their gilded horns already crimson.

Jason poised coolly a moment and skipped around the breaking men, jumping over a split shield. The bulls were chasing Apsyrtus's guards. One stood his ground. His spear broke in a bull's shoulder, then he was spitted like a chunk of meat.

Now, even the Colchis mob understood the trap Jason had avoided. They hated Apsyrtus and they roared with anger, pushing his guards back as they tried to scramble over the oak staves. Meanwhile, Jason sprinted like an antelope to the other end of the enclosure and vaulted back amongst us. We split the air with our yells.

Mud and manure plastered him from head to foot; he had bruises and a long gash from a stray spear. His face was smeared, his hair in sticky spikes, but he looked every part a warrior prince, his grin firmly in place. And despite the pain it must have caused, he bowed deeply to Aeetes.

'Great King, thank you for the lesson,' he said, his words exactly right.

Aeetes' face was wrinkled yellow, his watering eyes squeezed almost shut. 'Yes, it is useful to have another skill, Jason.' His voice was flat and serious; even now, I do not know if he knew of Apsyrtus's trap. 'We all need that, these are such troubled times.'

Aeetes remounted his horse and sat a moment, looking over our heads — considering, perhaps, whether to kill us now or later. 'Well, we shall show you where the Golden Fleece is.' He cackled softly; his watery eyes flashed at Medea now. 'Eh, daughter? That cursed hide that overshadows our kingdom, eh?'

There was a tittery edge to his words but no humour. He sat on his horse, thin shoulders hunched under the shaggy cloak. He was watching Medea and waiting for her answer. Abruptly he touched her cheek with the end of his riding crop — a gentle motion. Answer!

'Father, who knows what he will find. A quail flutters under your horse and you are thrown. Who spoke to the quail?'

Into Aeetes' watery eyes came a different flash, of respect — and caution. He was cutting at the shield of her very beliefs and she deflected it. She spoke again, her voice flat — hard as rocks waiting to splinter a keel.

'I will take Jason to the Golden Fleece. I hope that he wears sandals.'

King Aeetes looked at Jason. His bloodless lips drew back over his long yellowed teeth. 'Yes, Jason, wear sandals. Good advice.'

He looked from Medea to Apsyrtus, who glowered. Aeetes liked these games, I sensed; they were the stuff of kingship, like the ivory balls. He flapped a dry hand at them and turned away, his spearmen escort closing around him.

Apsyrtus ground out a single savage curse and leapt back onto his pony. He cantered after his father, not sparing a thought for his torn and bleeding men on the ground. Some had managed to escape, and the bulls, their rage gone, stood quietly among the victims and their broken weapons. Medea did not spare them a look either. She mounted and rode over, skirts bunched around her thighs, her bare brown legs gripping the pony's flanks. She turned it skilfully as she reached Jason and touched his sticky hair. Her nose crinkled.

'Jason,' she said, 'you stink.'

'I shall wash, lady,' he replied. 'Why must I wear sandals?'

Her brown hawk-look rested on him, neither warm nor cold. Her voice was the same way; light, though with the cold humour of her father.

'Sandals?' She gave Jason a long dark look. 'Because you will tread on the bones of those who went before.'

Still she did not smile. Her black ringlets tumbled around her shoulders as she swung the horse and cantered off. Always, always she was in control but I think her brown eyes sent a message to Jason. Anyway, he was still grinning as I poured a goatskin of water over his head and he scrubbed the muck away.

The crowd was streaming off too and Prontis came up, smiling; about to speak and the words went from his lips. He was looking over our shoulders, even his smile went. We turned.

To see the horsemen.

Perhaps twelve of them on a slight ridge in the distance. I didn't know how long they had been there, sitting shaggy little ponies with an ease that made them part of the animal. All wore high pointed caps and carried long lances. Their patchy fringed garments of horsehide and sheepskin gave them a tattered grace against the blue skyline. Prontis sucked in his breath and sighed.

'The horse tribes are early this year.'

As he spoke, the riders went. A flick of the reins and their little horses vanished in the long grass. Nobody else in the departing crowd seemed to have noticed them.

'Prontis,' Jason asked, 'will Aeetes give us the Fleece?'

'The Great King did not say he would give it to you.' Prontis spoke softly, his mouth tight. 'He only said he would show you where it was. The sleepless dragon is a more terrible guard than any bull.'

Jason did not reply. And I remembered Medea's answer — about wearing sandals. To walk over the bones of those who went before.

Chapter 15

Next morning, our guest-chamber door was open and the Amazons were gone. Prontis appeared, to say we had freedom of the city. Jason's cracked rib and bruises needed time to heal before the next test. So, after a breakfast of hard bread, sheep cheese and mare's milk, we went out to see the city.

Prontis said Aeetes was sick of the coughing illness and Prince Apsyrtus still sulking over the failure of his plan. We would not go to the shrine until the king was better. Then, said Prontis, we would have our chance to graze our shins on the bones of other seekers. Perhaps Aeetes was sick, muttered Jason to us. Or maybe he wanted us to see the wealth and power of his city.

Small groups only, said Prontis. I joined Jason again, with Butes, Castor and Pollux and Anceaus. At first we strolled casually down to the jetty where *Argos* was moored.

Just as casually, a group of the king's spearmen were lounging by the ship, passing an earthenware jug of beer and playing a game with little bone knuckles. Their blank looks warned us to go no further.

Argos appeared undamaged, so we walked along the wooden waterfront. Seagulls screamed overhead and the rich smell of drying fish came in the hot sunlight. The wharf was full of people — labourers, shipworkers and sailors, fishermen, even gangs of naked slaves. Nobody looked at us as we walked, and they worked on as though we did not exist. The people of Colchis knew change would come when Aeetes died. They saw us as part of this trouble.

So we went back into the city. Now the narrow streets were crowded. The smells here were human and animal and the noise louder. Some *Argos* men had found a wine shop and called to us. Zetes bounded happily over, followed by his brother and others. Jason kept walking and I followed, with Butes.

Here, the people did not ignore us quite as much. The Colchis women were bold-eyed and not so wrapped up, when standing in their own doorways. They had long hair and strong bold eyes. Their men were everywhere too, grim and watchful, long throwing knives stuck in their boots.

One woman squatted in her doorway, grinding barley. She was using a grinder — memory of Lemnos — but it wasn't that that made me shudder. A brown and green snake was coiled at her feet. All houses had their snakes, we learned, part worship and part rat-catcher. The men frowned at us but the women laughed and eyed us. They passed remarks about us in their own tongue that Prontis — grinning — refused to translate.

One threw Jason an apple and called something to him. The other women laughed and took it up, like a teasing chant. Prontis did translate this, 'Jason the Bull tamer.' So already, we thought, he was a legend. We found out later that it referred more to him rolling in the bullshit and meant something else.

At the other end of town was the market. It lay through those back, earth-bank walls that were not high enough to make the horse tribes angry. The market had created itself in only a few days, because rivers were the highways to Colchis. And to this market came traders from all over the unknown world.

Their craft all clustered now on the lake, like settling geese. Pot-bellied trading ships and slimmer high-pronged galleys not unlike ours. Strange ships too, with triangular sails. Ships like wooden castles. Even rafts and simple long dugouts. Ships of wood; ships of leather stretched over a wooden frame. Some even of bound reeds, bobbing light as ducks. All here to exchange their wares for Colchis gold.

There were red-haired tribesmen in thick woven cloth of green, blue and red patterns, who came from a far northern island where tin is mined. Other north-ice warriors in furs and horn-scaled armour, yellow-haired masters of the long axe, stared at us coldly with sea-blue eyes.

Others very different, tall brown-skinned men with strange hats of wrapped cloth, and hook noses, had come overland on huge beasts with two humps. Black-haired, golden-skinned men with slitted eyes, whose land was two years' journey away, sold the fine material that Medea's pink blouse was made of. Prontis said it was spun by a worm and we nodded, smiling. A half-Greek could not fool true Greeks with such tales.

And the unknown world had brought all its wares here. Pots, round or funnel-shaped with long or short spouts, three handles or none. Ingots of lead, tin, copper and silver; black stones that burned in fire like charcoal; the fur and hides of strange animals, fish and preserved meats, herbs; teeth, skulls, horns; cloth of all types and colours; jewellery of a strange clear stone with tiny insects imprisoned in it. Colchis people were here but they were not enough for a market this size. The merchants on these stalls were waiting for the horse tribes to come.

Every year this market came to Colchis, said Prontis. And so did the horse tribes, who followed the ripening ocean grass. They bartered gold and slaves for everything they did not have. Even salt fish was a delicacy to land-bound nomads. No wonder they did not want stone walls around Colchis. Perhaps then the gold tribute they received from the city would not be quite so forthcoming.

There was one item for sale I could not think anyone would want. From a land of skinny brown men, who dressed in white cotton, was a snake coiled in a wicker basket. It was dappled green and black with yellow cold eyes. The little bright-faced men demonstrated that it killed by crushing. In Colchis, the strange met from all directions and became normal.

So we returned to the guestrooms, our heads so crowded with puzzling and fantastic things that they nearly burst. Yes, Greeks could trade here; their swarming fish would feed us, their wares make us rich. First though — Jason muttering his thoughts aloud — we must break their dependence. They fear and depend on the horse tribes. He flung himself down on his sleeping rugs.

'Stone would keep the barbarians out,' he said.

You would not have to be a clever politician to know what he was thinking. I was sure Aeetes did, and Medea. The man who controlled that trade would be the most powerful in Greece. More so than any king. Jason lay, unsleeping, unconsciously letting his thoughts slip as he hummed a little tune. The same one that Heracles had hummed so long ago on Icolos quayside.

About a man with one sandal, marked for greatness by the Gods.

A week passed. We did not see King Aeetes in that time, although his guardsmen were everywhere. Always, there was a group beside *Argos*, giving us those stone blank looks if we went too close. Most of the crew found wine shops, and Zetes looked for women. At one time he had three husbands after him with their knives. Jason prowled around the city and through the market. Like all of us, he was dazzled by this sudden enormous display.

The fish market alone! My father often came back with empty nets. Here were herring, sardine, mackerel, fish we knew and many we did not. The belly of one long one held thousands of tiny black eggs. A grinning merchant gave me a handful; they were salt-tasting but good. We passed stacks and stacks of barrels, each crammed full. More in one season than we could take from our Greek seas in a year.

I was dazzled by the strangeness; Jason by the opportunity.

'It sets you thinking, does it not?' came a throaty voice behind us.

Weapons were not allowed in the market. Break that law and your head would be stuck on a pole to remind everyone else. But Medea's Amazons wore their bows and short swords openly. She walked towards us in that swaggering flaunting way. All gave way hastily. Around us, the different babble of tongues died away. Traders from frozen lands, deep jungles or deserts of sand, all were wary of Medea. Her voice became softer as she reached us, but was just as mocking.

'You did well with the bulls. Even the King was impressed and he has seen much.'

'I should like to thank Prince Apsyrtus for his part in the affair,' replied Jason, just as mockingly.

'Oh, forget the little boy. Soon he will not matter at all.' She glanced at me, Butes, Castor and Pollux, who were with Jason this day. 'Would you all care to come riding? I would consider it a great favour.'

'How could we refuse such a gracious invitation,' replied Jason, with a deep bow. 'I will have my crew summoned.'

'Oh, they can follow later,' she said, smiling. 'If they know where to look.'

Come now, she meant. She turned with a swirl of her skirts and led the way to some ponies. Behind her, the hubbub of the marketplace rose slowly

back to normal. We mounted and rode towards the grasslands.

The noise of Colchis market died away and we rode in silence. Medea led the way and we took a different route — to wooded foothills on the edge of the grass ocean. Medea paused on one of the ridges and pointed.

'There, Greeks. The first horse tribes come.'

I remembered those tattered riders outlined blackly on the ridge. Our hill-slope gently evened itself into the first swell of that vast grass ocean. And in the farmost distance was a smudging edge on the very curve of horizon itself; a dark edge that grew as we watched.

I remember the thick grass smell. The pony sweat and the hum of insects. The wind in our faces. And the silence — from morning till the sun was high. None of us thought about time passing, because the sight was so awesome. In the far distance the great black smudge was slightly closer. Now, distant, the wind brought voice-babble, horse noise, all the sounds of movement.

And as the fringe became closer, small groups of riders streamed ahead like threads unravelling from the edges of a huge dark blanket. The people of the grass ocean, their horses, their wheeled tents; a nation ten times larger than all Greece was on the move.

'Today my father rides out to meet them. Tonight they camp in the plains.' No mocking note in her voice now, as though that great mass of people could not be joked about. 'And tomorrow they come to market. So we have little time, Jason.'

She led the way again. This time away to where a thick belt of forest began. The land here was poor and rocky, the trees close set. And now as I rode, I saw carvings in stone; crude faces in the rocks and spiral white lines. On the tree trunks, more faces, buttocks and bulging bellies; the natural shape of the trees carved into the suggestion of something human. This was a Mother forest, a most sacred place, and we knew where Medea was taking us.

To the shrine of the Golden Fleece.

Then we waited, among another grove of thick oaks, until more riders came. Among them, in black cloak and hood, King Aeetes. He cocked his head on his shoulder, his thin lips pressed tight. His voice was light as the scratching of a dry leaf.

'You have seen the horse tribes, Jason. Would stone walls keep them out?'

'No, Great King,' replied Jason. It was true.

Aeetes gave his thin cold little titter, coughed and wiped a hand over his mouth. 'Soon I ride to greet them. Tomorrow we feast their leaders. But now there is family business.'

There was something cold and evil in the way he used those words, 'family business.' He glanced at Medea, motioning to the darker trees ahead. I noticed his guards kept from their long shadows. 'The test of the Fleece is a test for champions. Medea will show you. She knows the place well, do you not, daughter?'

'Yes, father,' she replied. 'I do.'

I tingled with great unease. Medea may have encouraged Jason to help her against Prince Apsyrtus. But she was a priestess of the Mother; something in her tone said this was wrong, badly wrong. Aeetes pulled all their strings, like the evil old puppet master he was.

He swung his horse around to go. His brown eyes actually rested on me a moment, a thin evil smile on his wrinkled old face. Maybe it was the scared look on mine. There was no humour in his smile, just a malicious satisfaction. He rode past and his troop followed. As they did, they expertly blocked Jason and me from the others; herding their ponies around, grabbing their bridles.

Castor yelled and so did Pollux. Jason silenced them with a wave. They were pulled away, looking back at us, till the dark trees hid them from view. I felt colder now and it was more than shadows. An Amazon grabbed my bridle, another took Jason's. Medea's face was expressionless again as she rode ahead, taking us further into those silent dark groves.

The trees closed more thickly and I could see why the guards kept from their shadows. All fear the Mother's cold touch. Close and dark now, breast and belly features shaped on them. More faces with wide eyes that stared out of the gloom. Fewer birds and colder shadows on the ground. Olive and oak trees twisted knobbly jointed branches like beckoning fingers. We were trespassers here.

Jason knew I was scared and he managed a smile. 'This will be interesting, Pylos,' he said in a low voice.

Medea turned, her own voice loud among the dark trees. 'No need to whisper, Jason. The Mother knows you are coming!'

That made it worse. Medea must be powerful to use the Mother's name so loudly. She began singing a little song in an unknown old-sounding tongue. A prayer to the Mother. Now there were offerings around us, all different, perhaps from women of different countries. Little clay pots, scraps of cloth were tied to branches. One tree was hung with jewellery — silver, bronze and copper — twinkling like dark frost. No thief would ever touch them. This place was deadly sacred. I felt her power, cold as a hand closing around my body.

Medea's pony whinnied as she reined abruptly on the stony lip of a small hollow. She dismounted, her face still expressionless.

'There, Jason. The Sacred Place of the Fleece.'

He dismounted and so did I, wanting to stay close. The leaves rustled underfoot like dry laughter. Behind us, the Amazons sat stock-still on their ponies. I had no idea what the Sacred Place would look like. In Greece, God places are splendid and full of riches — or you feel their anger.

This was like nothing I had seen.

The hollow deepened so that dark shadow filled it like a lake. There was enough overhead sun to outline a clutter of steep-roofed buildings, jammed and tumbling together at the end of the hollow. There was one small doorway; some little narrow windows. It squatted like a wooden beast in the shadows. Nine steep roofs — a sacred number, I remembered from somewhere.

'All different shrines to the Mother, built joined to each other.' It was as though Medea's voice caught the cold shadows. 'Through them is a sacred grotto, old to the Mother when the world was young. There is the Golden Fleece. The luck of Colchis.'

Not a sound came in the cold stillness. Even the breeze had stopped. Jason turned to her. 'Princess, I came for a golden fleece. Any one of those in the hill streams. Not this one. Support me with Aeetes and let us have a trading colony here. I will not take this Fleece.'

Medea just looked at him, her face like brown

stone. 'We are here, Jason. The Mother wills what will happen. And the guardian of the shrine. They are expecting you.' She slapped her little pony whip hard against her thigh, seeming to repress a shudder. 'Now go, the two of you, where others have gone.'

'Two?' I heard Jason ask and a chill went through my body. 'I will go alone.'

'Two of everything to the Mother's shrine.' Her voice was flat but she looked perplexed a moment as though great doubts were catching at her. Then the expression was gone as she looked at me, her brown eyes full of dark death. 'He must go too.'

She pointed her little pony whip straight at me.

Chapter 16

'Lord Jason,' I said, 'if I am going to die down there, I would like the answer to one question.'

'One question? Of course, Pylos,' he replied with just a trace of princely sarcasm.

It was early afternoon now. Medea had said we must wait an hour before going into the hollow. She had ridden away without a backward glance. The only sound we could hear was the slight rustle of laurel trees. No birds or animals. And the sense of being watched. Some of Medea's Amazons perhaps or the eye of that strange sleepless guardian. Perhaps just those images, looking from tree and rock.

'The Fleece is sacred to Medea, not Apsyrtus. But she contacted us, not he. We should be her enemy. He should be our friend.'

Jason was snapping a twig into pieces. He squinted up at the sun to see how the hour was passing. 'Medea is cleverer than her brother. He hates us, and perhaps she does. But she will use us to make the King doubt his son's judgment. That will give her more power.'

It sounded simple when he explained it. Of course Jason was used to noble ways — and devious, himself. I tried not to shiver and to speak normally. 'But what if we take the Golden Fleece. Will she try and kill us?'

'That is a second question,' replied Jason, 'but I will answer it. I think King Aeetes does want Greeks here. Our presence will make him more powerful. If I pass this test, the Gods are protecting me. So he will protect me from Medea.' He threw away the twig and looked at me. 'Pylos, you don't have to come.'

'Yes I do,' I said.

I was scared but I was Greek. And in Jason's crew. Jason just nodded but that was good. He stood up and dusted his hands, staring down the incline. He was serious but a little of the old grin was there.

'We can be thankful for one thing,' he said.

'What's that?' I asked.

'No rules,' he replied simply and led the way down.

I followed. It was like walking into cold water. Here would sacrifices be made — I could imagine Medea wielding a dagger — and in the undergrowth, the gleam of white bone. A large flat stone before the entrance was splashed with dark blood. Not more than a day old, with little black flies buzzing over it.

A fence enclosed the shrine. It was old, of rickety laurel poles; the gate leaned on leather hinges. It was only there to keep out wolves and dogs — they are no respecters of sacred places. Jason pushed the gate open easily. Something rustled and he skipped back as a little black snake slithered briefly into view.

'I think they're poisonous,' I said.

Jason took the hint and we approached the entrance from rock to rock. There was a smell to the air of things dead, things not belonging to the freshness above. As though the hollow were a soup ladle dipped into the ghostly half-light of the underworld. Another snake slithered into view and Jason stopped. I think we both had the same thought at the same time.

'I wonder how many snakes are inside,' he whispered.

'They're everywhere,' I replied, looking constantly around. 'Maybe, inside, the sleepless dragon eats them.'

Jason thought a moment. Prontis had assured us the dragon existed — and we had seen many strange things in Colchis. 'We have not heard it,' he said doubtfully.

'Maybe they make no noise.'

Jason grunted. 'Let's worry about the snakes first.'

He was right. We both wore cross-strapped leather sandals but, even with leggings, the snakes might slither up our legs and bite our thighs. Or snakes in the roof might drop on our heads. We would be dead long before the dragon had a chance to eat us.

'We have to keep above them,' I said.

Jason looked up at the sun. An hour to wait, one hour to get into the shrine, Medea had said. The hour was passing. 'Perhaps Hermes-Prankster will lend us his winged sandals.'

'What about over the roof?'

'Nine rooms,' said Jason. 'We would have to find the right one and somehow break inside. And still get to the ground.'

Over the ground. Somehow above it. Or swinging down from the roof. Images in my head. Thinking back to my seaside village, Cretan acrobats passing through on the way to a lord's feast. One of them, a little drunk, showing off. High-stepping down the beach where the boats were drawn up. Overbalancing in a pile of fish guts, grabbing the cross-tree of a mast. High enough to do that because he was on —

'Stilts,' I said.

Jason looked incredulous a moment. Then his sharp Greek wits took over. Keeping a careful eye for snakes, he beckoned me back to the fence. We pulled out some of the laurel poles. Medea had left us no weapons, but Jason had a knife strapped against his thigh. He smiled at me as he pulled it out, making the blade flash in the pale sunlight and shadow — the iron knife I had given him.

Half of our hour must have passed. I stood beside him and threw stones at every slither-sound in the undergrowth. He cut the poles to length and notched a section in each. A shorter length we bound to this as a foothold. We had nothing but the cross-straps of our sandals to use. That meant going barefoot in a place full of snakes. It was later afternoon now and the shadows were very cold.

Jason tested his stilts first. He was wobbly on them but had the balance of a born sailor. Soon he was walking and so was I. We staggered a little getting the balance; once our heads banged painfully together. Then Jason gritted his teeth and stumble-clopped in a determined line towards the shrine.

'Come on,' he said.

For a moment, I thought our stilts would be too high for the entrance. But Jason ducked under somehow and I followed. A stench of black stale air hit us. Some little light flashed. Mutton-fat lamps had been lit that day and spat their feeble yellow shadows from room to room ahead.

'Who lit them?' I asked.

Jason just shook his head. Later, we found out that the priestesses who attended the shrine had a special tolerance to snake bite; they took the poison in small doses from childhood. Right then it was a good question because the light showed a floor that hissed and slithered in a rush-work of entwined thin black shapes. My stilt leg jarred slightly and I looked down. A snake had already struck at it, just below my bare foot.

'I think this whole mass is the dragon,' muttered Jason.

Our eyes were accustomed to the gloom now. There was one door ahead but it led into two rooms; each into two more. Nine little rooms, each close and stifling, set with the same doors. Entwining carvings covered the dark walls. Little inset alcoves held statues, bulge-stomached statues, thin statues with long rope hair, even dolls in the neat flounced robes of the priestess.

All had wide eyes that followed us.

And as we moved, our stilts disturbed more than snakes; they rattled against the bones and rib cages of human skeletons. The skulls were missing. This was a bad dark place where nobody lived but the shrine guardians. Nine rooms in this almost-blackness was a maze; the yellow lamp shadows made it worse, not better. They made black shadows leap out of the darkness on either side. Jason whispered grimly, his breath hissing.

'First door.'

Nothing stopped him. Our stilts knocked together again, our heads banged painfully. The snakes hissed and spat below, their yellow venom splattering everywhere. They struck at our stilts again and again. Nor did they always wriggle clear fast enough. Sometimes the hissing ended with a thud as a stilt-leg came down. Jason wobbled slightly, but laughed.

'Medea's sleepless "dragon" seems annoyed!'

Another problem now. Whoever built this dark, close honeycomb of wood had roofed it with wooden beams, set with wooden pegs. Now a thickspun mat of cobwebs clung to it. Through it scuttled the owners, hundreds of tiny black spiders. They were not venomous, luckily. But our heads disturbed their nests and they scuttled out in savage defence, biting sharp as needles, over cheeks, neck and shoulders.

So we went from room to room, into that thick unwholesome stench, into the black-dancing shadows, each dark place so alike. It was easy enough to get lost, and once we back-clumped over crushed snakes, retracing our steps. Jason stopped, whistling, looking around and nodding towards another doorway.

I staggered now, coughing, nearly overwhelmed and trembling. The snakes hissed more strongly and the cobwebs were thick as a grey cloud. Jason's hand shot out, grabbing my shoulder tightly a moment. The horror rose in my throat like vomit but I somehow nodded back. He clumped on before me, through another doorway. I stooped, still unsteady, my head hitting the low lintel. Ahead, Jason balanced, looking back, hissing sharper than any snake.

'Pylos! This is the last room!'

He grinned. And even in this moment, I had to admire him. Jason the prince always kept his dignity. Even lurching on stilts, his brown hair dusted grey-thick with cobwebs, a spider hanging off the end of his nose. He blew it away, clumped further through and somehow managed to turn and point at the same time.

'Here!' he hissed, sharp with excitement. 'The Golden Fleece!'

Who but Jason would have clumped so confidently inside? So confident that I had to clump after him. A snakehead crushed under my stilt. I stalked in, ducking my head, sweeping away cobwebs and black spiders, poking one out of my ear, looking around. Another room — as dark and bad-smelling as the others. This was a very old room; the far wall was the natural rock face of the grotto; the rock lines carved to a staring Mother face.

A single clay lamp guttered; a presence glimmered like a pinned octopus.

The Golden Fleece. Splayed on the wall, the tufted wool stiffened into peaks like wavetips of beaten gold. It did not gleam but smouldered, full of rich dark glints. This fleece had been put in the mountain rivers many years ago when the world was younger and the waters richer with their bright specks of gold. Now it was stiff with gold, the head a shaped skull of pure gold and golden twirling horns.

It was natural, made of things natural — the most splendid thing I had ever seen.

Jason clumped over and put out his hand. His fingers touched the stiff gold points of wool. Then from below came a sharp cutting hiss, much louder than any other snake noise in the guttering shadows, and something moved.

Something that was thick and coiling, huge as a true dragon.

It was bigger, much bigger than the small one I had seen in Colchis market; traded from somewhere in the unknown world; the same dappled green and black patterned scales, large cold yellow eyes; thicker and longer than *Argos*'s mast. It uncoiled, full of hate and anger. I gasped, choking on the dry bad stench of the place.

'They must have brought it here young!'

Jason interrupted me patiently. 'Shall we discuss it later?'

He took a backward step. His head banged on a roof beam and more spiders fell. The big snake reared up — looking even bigger — and struck. Jason put out a stilt-leg, propping himself against the wall of the shrine. The snake was already coiling up his stilt, snapping the tough laurel shaft like a rotten twig. I remembered how that brown-skinned man gestured, closing his hands.

'Crushing!' I yelled. 'It kills by crushing!'

Jason balanced on one stilt. It slithered quickly up around his legs and lower body. Its tail took firm anchor around the stone base of the Mother statue and began to crush. Jason stabbed with his iron dagger, but a stunning blow from the snakehead knocked it to the floor. He beat it with his fists — as well strike Heracles with a feather.

'Pylos!' he yelled.

Me, the fisher boy. His only chance. The snake flickered in my direction. Its mast-thick coils wound snugly tight around Jason's body, beginning to crush. Jason's mouth opened in the first gasp of death. All of this so quick — it took less time than it takes a sail to fill with wind.

I lurched over and tore down the Fleece from its hooks. As I did, my stilts nearly went from under me. The Fleece crackled, thick and metallic, as I threw it at the snake. The squat head was still turning, flinching as the Fleece struck it. The golden ram's head broke off. The thick crushing coils lessened. Jason kicked hard, roaring like a lion. He and the snake fell to the ground; he kicked clear, free only a moment, the snake already turning.

'Ram skull!' he shouted.

Only Jason could think so quickly. I grabbed the ram skull, swinging it by one golden horn, throwing it at the snake. It was light, only a hollow gold-plated skull after all. But one horn-tip caught the snakehead, puncturing one yellow eyeball, spilling a pale fluid.

A moment; it was long enough for Jason to grab his broken stilt leg — a good club — and with a spirit worthy of Heracles, he battered the snake's head to pulp. It collapsed in twitching coils. Jason grabbed the Fleece, hopping back on his single stilt before one of the smaller snakes could get him. He grinned, gasping with the pain of his bruised body, propped against the wall.

'No going out, Pylos.'

There was not. Jason could not hop on one stilt and handle the big Fleece at the same time. So, with the broken half of his stilt-leg, Jason hammered up at the roof beams. They soon gave way at the joints. Just as the solid gold ram skull was hollow, this temple was rotten with long ages — an illusion of strength like all Colchis. Soon, the splintered roof-tiles let in a bar of late afternoon sunlight.

It showed the snake, its broken head oozing grey brains, broad coils still twitching among white bones. Medea's sleepless pet, sleeping forever. Little black snakes still hissed among the bones and a collection of skulls in one corner. Daring, I bent over and scooped up Jason's iron knife. Then we climbed out onto the steep roof.

Jason pulled me up after him. He rolled the gold Fleece into crackly folds. The gold skull he left to be slithered over by the little black snakes. We had come for power, not gold. Jason pushed his knife into his belt and gave me that big loose grin — the grin of someone always in love with life.

'Pylos, the best thing I ever did was take you on this voyage.'

And that was the best praise I ever had. There, on the broken Colchis shrine roof. I grinned back and my cheeks burned. Being a ship's boy among heroes, the fighting and the terror — all washed away like the breaking of a single Hellespont wave. Just that moment and Jason already looking around.

'Let's go.'

We slid down the roof onto the ground and quickly outside the old palisade. Good to be away from that doom-ridden place of snakes and power. And walking back up the hollow we were equals. We had dared together.

At the top, he became Jason the prince, again. It was not personal; there is something in princes that they cannot change.

Behind us, the steep little roofs of the shrine were reddened by the late sun, the dark shadows as cold as ever. We began walking back through the forest; through the laurels whispering and touching us with their dry fingers. Even walking like this seemed unreal — too easy. We had robbed the Mother shrine and she never forgave.

Jason thought so too. We passed one old oak, deeply cleft in the middle. He paused, thought, and stuffed the sheepskin inside. For the moment it was better hidden. I knew what he was thinking. Maybe, for a time, we could pretend the Fleece was not taken. Jason — always thinking ahead.

Jason was right to think that. Somebody did intend to stop us, no matter what her father decreed. And of all the bad things we left behind, a worse thing lay ahead. Through the thinning trees, we met Medea and her Amazon bow women.

We saw them before they saw us. Medea had her back turned, the late sun like sacrificial bloodlight around her. She was looking at what lay on the ground before her. We stopped and looked too. At the end of this day, full of horrors, it was the worst thing we could have thought of.

King Aeetes and his spearmen escort. All lay tumbled on the ground, overwhelmed by that first volley of arrows. Arrows sticking everywhere, in the horses, in the men, in their shields. Thickly on the ground. All driven deep at short range, nine in Aeetes and his horse alone. His wrinkled face upturned, his sharp little smile fixed in place by the arrows that pinned his body to the ground.

Medea turned. Jason held out his empty hands.

Her eyes shone without joy as she looked him up and down. Clever Jason had overlooked the specks of gold on his kilt, his hands and his breast. Her face grim in the reddening afternoon, vengeful as befitted a daughter of the Mother.

'Greetings, shrine thief,' she said.

Around her, the Amazons were calmly fitting arrows to bowstrings, the red sun flashing on their sharp arrowheads ...

Less pitiless than the look in Medea's eyes.

Chapter 17

Medea and her Amazons were waiting there to kill us. Whatever Aeetes decreed, whatever she felt for Jason, her first duty was to the Mother. But when they came to this killing ground, they found the bodies. King Aeetes wanted the Fleece too.

Jason and I had already seen the arrows sticking in Aeetes and his men. They did not come from the Amazon bows.

They were shorter and black-feathered.

'My dear little brother returned with a troop of nomad bowmen,' said Medea. 'Perhaps fifty, he could not afford to hire more than that.'

'Where are the men who came with us?' asked Jason sharply.

'All your crew are safe in Colchis,' replied Medea bitterly, 'safer than you would be, if —' she broke off but her meaning was clear. Finding the body of Aeetes saved us. A greater battle than revenge on two shrine breakers awaited her.

'Can you fight Apsyrtus?' asked Jason.

Medea ran a hand through her tangly black hair. 'If I strike soon,' she replied, thinking hard. 'The King's guard will rally to Apsyrtus.' Of course they would, Apsyrtus claiming Amazon arrows had slain Aeetes. 'Together their forces will outnumber my Amazons.'

'And fifty Greek pirates —' shouted Jason, 'who will fight like ten times their number for a cargo of gold?'

Medea suddenly laughed. 'Enough gold to sink you!'

The wind whipped her black ringlets as she re-mounted. An Amazon brought up horses. Jason sprang onto the saddle, I was shoved onto mine. Then we were riding in a thunder of hoofbeats. I hung on somehow, grabbing both reins and mane, the wind beating my face.

Medea thought as quickly as Jason did. Strike fast — and fifty Greek warriors would make a difference. That was the only reason she spared us. As we galloped into the gathering dark, to one side, sparkling yellow dots scattered like endless fallen stars; camp fires, marking the black host of the nomads.

Apsyrtus was chancing all in a wild gamble. Kill his father and blame his sister. He worshipped the same gods as the horse tribes; they would see him as a better puppet. Easier to control than Medea. She was supposed to die in the same ambush but took a different path to the meeting. The fight was against her, but Medea's blazing spirit would not allow Colchis to be taken without a battle.

We rode past the abandoned market. Stalls were overturned and torn awnings flapped in the evening sky. The merchants had withdrawn to their ships, clustering midriver like frightened ducks. There were flames in Colchis and the rattling sounds of battle, but it was not their fight. Medea grabbed a spear from one of her escorts and urged her pony ahead. Black hair flying, she galloped into the city.

The gates opened. Some of Apsyrtus's guards were looting a wine shop instead of attending to their duty. One staggered out, jug in hand. I will never forget his pop-eyed horror as Medea's spear caught him in the throat. He fell under our hooves, the spear snapped and she pulled out her sword.

More soldiers ahead went under our hooves, their spears clattering. Here lay the bodies of townsfolk who would not have supported Apsyrtus; Prontis, with a spear through him. And now, short stocky men in horsehair capes and pointed caps scattered quick as sparrows when they saw us coming; the hired nomad bowmen, who plainly considered their work done. Medea reined in, Jason beside her.

'Our crew will be shipside with *Argos* or still at the palace,' he said. '*Argos* first; I will go there. Pylos —'

He broke off. But I could think fast too. If the *Argos* crew were at their guest-chamber, Medea would not persuade them to move. So I would have to go. The fight noise was louder ahead, but I nodded. We had been through too much, fear was long gone. Jason swung his pony and set off down the street that led to the quayside. A sharp word from Medea and two Amazons followed. Guardsmen were there, I glimpsed Jason's sword rise and fall — then my reins were grabbed again. We were riding to the palace. Now, suddenly, the clangour of real battle began. In the palace square.

The rest of Medea's Amazons were ringed around the centre pillar. Some shot their short bows, others levelled their spears; some on the ground, others kneeling and bleeding. They yelled their battle cries as the king's guards and Apsyrtus's men ringed them in turn, jeering, daring them to attack. They had their own dead and wounded, though, and dared not close.

Medea gave a high yowl of fury. Astride her pony,

skirts bunched, she charged into the soldiers. They scattered in surprise. Medea's embattled Amazons raised a yell. They charged out of their encircling litter of dead and the fight broke up into little groups. A guard in front thrust his spear. My pony went down; two Amazons attacked him from behind.

Ahead, Medea threw herself onto the ground, the others followed. The ponies stampeded, their high frenzy adding to the din. More guards were running into the square and from the high palace entrance. I grabbed up a sword, the handle smeared with blood. The wooden paving stones of the square were dark with blood. No sign of our men, no chance of getting into the palace. The streets around us were blocked with more guards.

This was where we must stand and fight.

Medea shouted orders, ringing her Amazons back around the pillar. The guardsmen bunched and attacked against spears, arrows and shields. Medea was among the foremost, sword in both hands and screaming insults. I was jammed near her, Amazons on either side, no hope now of the *Argos* men. They would be fighting at the quayside or even setting sail — would Jason leave without me? The thought filled me, not with fear, but with battle frenzy.

Two guardsmen made for Medea. I slashed at one, making him skip. Medea and I were thrown together; I smelled her body sweat and perfume oils. The spear, aimed at her, caught my arm. I lunged again, my sword cutting the edge of his oxhide shield, into his neck. He staggered, blood spurted over Medea as she chopped down the second one. Another swirl of fighting swept us apart.

More guardsmen were tramping into the square, their shields locked, spears level. Amongst them, gleaming in his bronze-scale armour, was Apsyrtus. Medea screamed over at him, 'Ah, little brother, come for some real fighting?'

'Kill the witch woman and the assassins of our king!' he shouted back.

Now the battle locked to full fury, roaring like a storm at sea. In such a storm, you cannot keep your feet unless you are skilled. Some five hundred of Aeetes' guards and Apsyrtus's men were in the square. Medea's Amazons were less than two hundred. There were torches on brackets around the square. The red fire of a burning building — that and the pale moon overhead lit the battle scene as the two sides clashed together. When brother met sister, no quarter was asked and none given.

So the battle storm caught me. I was jerked off my feet at first. I fought because there was nothing else; it became a mad joy to cut and slash and not care about being hurt. Let the blood run, let the storm noise grow louder. Just fight — fight! An Amazon beside me was jerked up on a spear. Another flung herself on the spearman, stabbing at him. The last arrows shot, the line of spears pressed, battle closed around the high centre totem.

Medea's women locked their little leather shields and fought without giving way. The ground was slippery as a ship's deck in storm, with blood and bodies. A sword slashed at me. I clashed it sideways, the flat blade banging on my shoulder. Around me, as their numbers lessened, the Amazons were forced back. Now Apsyrtus brought in more bowmen, their arrow quivers full. They began to shoot.

The Amazons stood, their faces grimy and stubborn above their shields — little shields that gave small protection against arrows — and they began to fall. Clutching shafts, groaning, some toppling dead. The ranks closed, then closed again. Medea stood in full view, her blouse torn across, her skirts bedraggled with blood, sword in hand. But no arrows went near her. Apsyrtus was saving his sister for something special.

I was still jammed between two Amazons, my sword heavy and useless as a gold bar in my hand, holding up a little shield, stuck with three arrows. Another arrow flight came, cruel as death. Another arrow stuck in my shield, one tore past my ear. My warm blood flowed, but the women did not move, so I did not. I was Greek — a man now — and death is part of life. It was death because the tramp of feet came again, more warriors marching to the assault.

The Amazons locked their arrow-studded shields; the arrows driven with such force that shields were pinned to arms. I was weak and dizzy; my arm ached from thrusting; wondering if death would hurt. The new warriors tramped up but their armour flash was different in the firelight, their battle shout strangely familiar — a chant. My senses spinning, I knew that chant. The rowing song of *Argos*!

Jason and the Argonauts!

I was on my knees and staggered back to my feet. A last arrow whizzed past, the Amazons gave back. Then the ranks of Apsyrtus's men shuddered as a bronze force crashed in behind them. Only fifty Greeks, but these were champions and heroes, raised to battle craft since birth. Marching close in full armour, each with sword and two throwing-spears, shields overlapping, they were in the mood for a good bloody fight. Their battle chant roared out again.

Let oars slap water — stroke!

Twenty-five javelins flew. Guardsmen fell; some struck from the back, others as they turned. Our first line backed, the second came forward and cast their spears. Stroke! Apsyrtus's men were in confusion as our first line came forward again in a deadly battle-step. Twenty-five more spears flew.

Stroke!

A javelin whizzed over Apsyrtus's head, another in his horse; he went down among his men. They broke as the Greek line crashed into them. Step forward, swords out, stamp the foot and thrust!

Stroke!

Shields still locked, eyes glaring under bronze helmet-rims. Step forward, swords out, stamp the foot and thrust! Stroke! Now they crashed and broke the guards like a bronze battering ram. Medea ran forward, waving her sword. Born fighter that she was, she knew the crisis teetered either way.

'Charge!' she shouted. 'Forward!'

She ran forward and her Amazons followed. Even the wounded stumbled after them. Apsyrtus's men still outnumbered us but there was no rally; they could not fight that bronze warrior machine that killed to unknown shouts. Now they were breaking and I last glimpsed Apsyrtus yelling curses as he was swept away by panicked men into the narrow wooden alleys of the city. Within minutes only the dead remained. There were no wounded, because Amazon swords saw to that.

Yes, no quarter when brother met sister.

Jason came forward. He was splashed all over with blood — shield, sword and armour — but looked splendid, as though out of legend. He fought his way down to *Argos* and they all fought their way to us. Anceaus grinned and Zetes waved his sword. 'Hey, boy, stayed with the women, eh? Anything missing?'

They laughed and I laughed back. Jason grabbed my hand and squeezed tight. There was respect from the others, Butes slapped my shoulder. I winced from the spear jab but happily. The hours fighting in the square, the blood and pain from my wounds were worth it; more than ornaments of gold.

Medea did not laugh. She looked at Jason, her face a mask. Blood ran from a gash in her arm and a spear cut in her side. Her black hair was sticky with blood where an arrow grazed her forehead; her voice was hoarse from screaming insults. She told her captains to picket the square and see to their wounded. Then she turned and walked up to the palace entrance. On the top step, she beckoned us to follow. Her Amazon bodyguard did, and most of *Argos's* crew.

'No looting!' muttered Jason.

'Us?' replied Castor, rolling his eyes in pretended horror.

Inside, the huge wooden throne room was empty. The torches still burned in their bronze brackets but all the councillors would be shut in their homes.

On the throne was the ram's-horn crown with its crest of eagle feathers. Perhaps Apsyrtus had been trying it on when the Amazons attacked. Medea picked up the crown and tore off the eagle feathers; the gods of wind and storm no longer ruled in Colchis. She turned to face us.

'The proper way of doing this must come later.'

She placed it on her head and sat down. Her sticky tangled hair hung to her shoulders; her clothes were torn and bloodstained. And she sat like a queen. Even her voice was different when she spoke, staring over our heads as Aeetes had done.

'You will have your gold, Jason. Enough to convince your little city king, Pelias. But you leave the Golden Fleece. Now go.'

No thanks and a cold lingering stress on the now. Even my tired wits were sharp enough to take that hint. As I turned, Medea slipped off a gold arm ring and threw it to me. I caught it, still sticky with her blood.

'You took a spear wound for me. A queen pays her debts.'

Heavy gold too — enough to buy a fishing boat, a wife and some goats. I followed Jason and our men outside as more Amazons filed into the palace. The sounds of battle were gone as both sides rested now. Anceaus tore a strip off my tunic and bound up the arm-cut.

'First battle scar, Pylos!' he said, grinning. I grinned back. It was the first time he'd used my name.

'We sail in the morning,' said Jason.

In a body, we marched back through the narrow

streets. Now the citizens were out, forming lines with leather buckets. The people of a wooden town must be skilled fire-fighters; already the blaze was lessening. There was no sign of Apsyrtus's men; they had fled outside the city walls and so had their prince. Medea, as queen, could order the town militia to bar the gates. Apsyrtus was finished and tomorrow we would have our cargo of gold. We could leave.

I ached all over. There was sticky blood plastering me and even those spider bites, from long long before, still itched. I tramped with the others and remember seeing *Argos*, the wooden jetty under my feet. Then somehow it wobbled. Zetes' strong arm caught me as I fell into blackness.

Chapter 18

I woke at dawn to bustle and movement in the ship. Somebody had bandaged my wounds but I was stiff and sore; my head ached with hoofbeats of fire. But the others were working, so I scrambled up too. We untied ropes, checked the rigging and sail, then had breakfast. Bread, cheese and olives; simple enough, but I ate with them, as one of them. I was never prouder.

Soon, a group of town councillors appeared, with laden donkeys. They brought our gold and from their looks, did not like to. But some of Medea's Amazons were with them and she ruled Colchis now. So, unwillingly, their gold was passed over. More gold than I have ever seen in my life. A full ship's cargo.

Gold in flat ingots, leather bags of gold dust, a bale of those gold-stiff fleeces. Gold in rings, brooches, cloak pins and belt buckles, hammered into fantastic images. Gold necklaces, gold earrings. So much gold that *Argos* groaned and the waters slopped close to the oar-line.

Half our company stood guard and Jason took the other half with him — to meet Medea and return the Fleece. Otherwise we would not have left Colchis alive. No matter what Medea's debt to us, her first duty was to Rhea-Mother.

The last fires burned down as the sun rose. The blood was dry on the wooden streets; the militia assembled in their bad-fitting armour, clutching their weapons clumsily like the tradesmen they were. But they outnumbered Apsyrtus's scattered forces and would fight to keep their city from further damage. Medea had won.

She wore another of those flounced skirts and her blouse was a light blue, stitched with silver thread in moon-sickle shapes. Over it she wore a gold-scaled sleeveless tunic, with a heavy gold circlet on her black hair, set in front with a large serpent head. Red-jewel eyes flashed at us, as though with hate. Her own brown eyes had no expression at all. She greeted us in the same flat way she had dismissed us last night.

We rode outside the city. The gates were manned by militia who averted their eyes from Medea. Some still believed she had murdered her father, even though his body lay in the palace, the nomad shafts there for all to see. Medea sensed their hostility, I am sure, and ignored it.

She rode ahead, in silence. We had saved her city and she would need Greek allies. Also, we had dese-crated her shrine and, indirectly, caused the death of her father — enough reason for her to take what-ever vengeance she liked. But she had given her word and, in her way, she liked Jason. But liking and duty were torn in different directions.

The Fleece still lay where Jason had hidden it, gleaming golden, wet with the morning dew. Her face still closed, Medea rolled it up and tied it across her saddle. She remounted, sunlight flashing gold in her dark hair, and looked over to Jason.

'Will you return to Colchis?' she asked.

'You know that I will,' replied Jason.

173

'Be it on your own head,' she replied. 'There is too much that I love and hate in you.'

Mix tin with copper and you make a better metal: bronze. Jason and Medea were like that. They quickly became part of each other; they were truly strong for each other but only because of the moment. Like the mix of metals, like two flames joining. She wanted to love him and she wanted to kill him. And here, in the forest of Rhea-Mother, our fate still hung. Then a new expression came into Medea's eyes.

She made a small noise and knelt quickly. She pressed her ear to the ground, listening intently. She looked up, puzzled, thinking; not liking what she realized, a hand still flattening the grass as though sensing unseen tremors beneath.

'Listen,' she whispered.

For long moments we heard nothing. Then the smallest noise, the faint faraway sound of very distant thunder. Like the first swell of a very powerful wave. Medea sprang onto her pony and galloped ahead to the ridge, her brown-clad Amazons following instantly, the rest of us further behind. Before us, she reined her pony motionless, as though waiting. But she was not thinking about us and did not turn as we came up. She was looking at what lay ahead.

In the distance was a broad black line like a slow-sweeping wave. This wave covered the green grass as far as we could see in either direction. Little shaggy nomads on their little shaggy ponies, thousands and thousands of them. They were trotting slowly, not having to gallop. The sheer flood of their movement would be enough. Like a wave over sand, Aeetes had said; this wave would sweep through all Colchis.

We all knew where Apsyrtus had fled.

'The horse tribes have never interfered in Colchis,' said Medea.

'They have now,' replied Jason simply.

Apsyrtus must have gone straight to the horse tribes; perhaps told them that Colchis had closed its gates, denied its tribute; that Greeks were taking over the kingdom. Whatever the reason, they were moving. Slowly it seemed, but covering the ground to the city.

Medea's lips were pressed white, black hair whipping around her face. It meant the end of her reign; she knew that. The Colchis militia would not stand against those many thousands; already her quick mind was thinking ahead. So, the Fleece on her saddle, she led us back to Colchis at the hard gallop.

The slow approaching thunder of the horse tribes had already been heard. The city gates were open, the town militia gone; their weapons scattered, clattering under our hooves on the wooden streets. They were shuttered in their homes to wait out the coming storm.

Medea's Amazons were massed by the harbour. Already the thunder was louder as though the horse tribes were coming to the gallop. Medea slid off her horse, shouting to her captains. 'I must go with the Greeks. But I will return. Scatter by the market and harbour; they won't follow.'

Her senior captain was a tall woman with reddish hair clipped very short, her eyes as blue as her tattoo marks. 'Queen,' she said, 'they will be through this city before you clear the harbour. They will follow.' She was right. On all sides were those sleek Colchis galleys and Apsyrtus had more than enough men for a pursuit. 'We can hold them in the streets for a time.'

'Do as I tell you!' snapped Medea.

'No, Queen,' replied the woman. 'It is better if we hold them in the streets.'

Medea struck her, hard. 'You are sworn to obedience!'

The captain just smiled. 'Queen, Daughter of the Mother, we are sworn to the death.' She had to raise her voice now, over the hoof thunder. 'And death is upon us.'

And as though this were already decided, another Amazon prodded Medea in the back with her spear butt. Just hard enough to pitch her headfirst into *Argos*. She landed on Calais and Butes and rolled over, gasping, frenzied; the only time I ever saw her out of control.

'Cast off!' shouted Jason. 'Oars!'

Argos backed away. I was on the stern deck, watching the Amazons. Strange, but it was the first time I saw them as people, not a faceless bodyguard. Some young and round-cheeked; one with a scarred stern face; a thin-cheeked woman, mouth shut hard against the pain of a bandaged forearm; one smiling quietly, one with a tear on her cheek; none looked scared.

They raised their swords in salute and turned back into the city. I think they were chanting a battle song, but it was lost in the hoofbeat thunder now shaking all Colchis. The gates shut behind them.

Medea walked up to the stern like a stiff, tired,

old woman. She sat beside me. Nobody spoke but we strained hard. Jason looking to the city, then to Medea. We were listening to the hoofbeat wave that rose to even louder thunder as we rowed away. Medea sat white-faced, hair straggling around her glaring eyes, hugging the Fleece tight to her body.

Now the thunder-wave drowned out our oar beats, so loud that it was the only noise in the world. Suddenly it crashed and faltered as though hitting a rock. For minutes the wave crashed hard on the rock, then swelled again as though the rock was broken. We rowed on in silence. After only a week, the oar blades seemed unfamiliar in our hands. We sweated and it was the only time I saw tears on Medea's cheeks.

'Those women,' grunted Pollux quietly as he strained on his oar. 'What Spartans they would have made!'

There was no emotion on Medea's pale face now; that made it all the more frightening. Jason came up and put his hand on her shoulder. She did not move but to push her hair back from her face. I saw her earrings for the first time — big silver sickles in her black ringlets. She touched one and pricked her finger on its sharp point, looking at the red bead of blood it raised.

Colchis lay clear in the bright morning light behind us. We were outside the river mouth before the gates banged open and the nomad flood spilled out. It swirled as though a black land tide was scouring all Colchis; washing its tattered fringes out onto harbour-side and jetty. It lapped and wavered on the waterside; a land flood could go no further. But

177

soon, among the line of galleys was oar-movement and masts being raised.

Apsyrtus was in pursuit.

There is a saying among sailors that a stern chase is a long one. The blood of Medea's Amazon guards saved us that day; the sea wind caught our sail before those long black galleys cleared the river mouth. And even with a full sail, we rowed for extra speed but *Argos* moved slowly, with a bellyful of gold. We only just kept ahead. And slowly, through the long day, they cut our lead.

Medea said nothing. She crouched in the stern, the rolled Fleece hugged tight in her arms. Lips moving, as though she were muttering prayers — or curses. If prayers for our success, they were not heard. The first galley closed to ten lengths behind *Argos*, when night fell.

We rested on the oars. Then rowed and rested again. Sensible sailors stop each night and pull up on a beach, but this was no time to be sensible. Jason had the steering oar; we slept, then rowed. I pulled with the others, proud that I no longer ached.

Even after that week in Colchis, my hands were still callused.

'Will they follow us?' I asked Butes.

'Easy enough to follow that.' He wagged his bearded chin upwards, to our big white sail gleaming in the moonlight. 'Considering how dearly brother and sister love each other ... Yes, they will.'

At the steering oar, Jason and Medea heard us. Nothing was said, though, and the night passed. Dawn touched the sky in pale coral pink, the sea dark, the rising sun touching it to a blue-green. The Colchis galleys, behind us, were lean dark jackals, and closer. By mid-morning they would be upon us.

Long before then, the first arrows came on board.

They stuck in our sail and on our sides. We slung shields on our backs but they kept striking. Anceaus was a target, now on the steering deck. He skipped and swore, yelled angrily as an arrow cut under his armpit. There were islands within sight now, low and rock-bound and no place to stop.

More arrows came. Even more, as the other galleys caught up, and Orpheus yelled in horror as one cut the string of his lute bag. Anceaus swore a whole string of foul oaths as one stuck under his knee. Like jackals nipping, little by little they would weaken us, bite at our heels, wear us down before closing to board.

Jason and Medea talked in the bow. A low intense conversation. Then abruptly he raced down to the stern, looking back at the foremost black craft, now a galley's length behind. He put up both hands, yelling for us to ease oars. The lead galley nosed closer. Apsyrtus, in helmet and bronze-scale armour, stood up in the bow.

'Greeks, do you want life or death?' he yelled.

'What sort of answer do you expect?' shouted Jason back. We could still laugh.

Apsyrtus smiled like a weasel, his galley nosing closer. 'I have no quarrel with you. Give me Medea — or throw her overboard, if you think she will float long enough for us to get her.'

'Why do you want her?' shouted Jason. 'She is beaten.'

'My kingship must start with a good sacrifice,'

yelled Apsyrtus back. Gold hawk feathers gleamed on his helmet. 'One that will impress the horse tribes.'

Medea stood up, her eyes flashing like a fury-spirit. 'You little milk-sopping mongrel! You brought the horse tribes to Colchis! They were guests and now they are overlords!'

'Yes, and they don't worship your old mother of mud and trees,' shouted Apysyrtus back. 'Her days are over!'

Unwise, I thought. Rhea-Mother is more powerful than a Colchis princeling. Medea joined Jason at the stern. Again, no words were said — just the uncanny feeling they knew each other's thoughts. Then Jason yelled back.

'I want the Golden Fleece!'

'That scrap of worm-eaten hide?' Apsyrtus laughed, balancing against the roll of his ship; thinking he had Jason's measure. 'Take it and give me the bitch-priestess.'

Medea glared at Jason when he asked for the Fleece. Now she screamed, slashing her hand at his face. 'No! You promised to protect me!'

Her fingernails left four red marks down his cheek. He slapped her back, hard enough to make her collapse onto the deck. She suddenly looked foolish and dismayed. Jason's face was grimmer and harder than I had ever seen it before as he looked around. One of those little rock-bound islands was close. He pointed to it.

'There! You and I will make the peace oaths there. Without weapons. You can trust Greek honour.'

'What sort of answer do you expect?' yelled Apsyrtus back and his men laughed. Six of his black galleys bobbed close to us now.

'Those are the terms if you want her without fighting.' Jason kicked Medea to underline his words. 'Your galleys still outnumber us, Prince. No need to be afraid.'

Apsyrtus talked among his men then held up his hand. He agreed; he had to, showing his men he was not afraid. And his galleys did outnumber us.

So we rowed near the island and threw out our anchor stone. The Colchis galleys rowed to the far side of the island; two remained to watch us. All of us were silent, curious, not wanting to interfere; watching Jason.

He packed a little bag with a flask of wine, bread and salt. He and Apsyrtus would taste these, the tokens of sacred honour that no prince would break. He did not look at Medea again. She looked at him though, her lips parted as though the curses were streaming silently out. He wore a linen tunic and carried no weapon.

'I would sooner trust one of their snakes than that prince,' said Pollux loudly amid a murmur of agreement.

Jason ignored this, glancing at me. 'Pylos, wait with Medea on the beach. Everyone else, stay here.'

There was another loud mutter; men slapped their thighs in protest. Jason took no notice. We were closer to the island now and he jumped between the oars, into the water. He splashed to the beach, up to the ridge and was lost from sight.

Medea followed without protest. She was going to her death but she went like a queen. To the bad slow death by torture that her brother would give her. Jason, the only one oath-bound to help her, would hand her over. Our men watched in silence as she jumped over and waded ashore without a backward look. Had she called to us, we would have helped. I think at that moment, all of us thought differently about Jason.

I followed her ashore. She hitched up her skirts and sat on some rocks. Still I had the impression that nothing mattered. The horse tribes would make the laws in Colchis now. The balance of power was gone.

I followed her to the rocks. I sat near her. Then I noticed something that set an ice dagger cutting in my stomach — faint circling lines on one of the stones; wide eyes on another; a third shaped like a full breast. Here Medea sat, her dark eyes full of witchfire. Jason may have deserted her but she still had power.

The ice dagger cut deeply into me. I had made to sit but did not. This place, like the skeleton cave, like all Lemnos, like the Fleece grove — all this place was sacred ...

To Rhea-Mother; this was her island.

Chapter 19

Medea sat on one of the rocks and composedly arranged her skirts. *Argos* rocked in the bay. I sat on a rock too — after making sure it had no markings. The island was sleepy, hot and silent. By now Jason and Apsyrtus would be meeting. The sun beat more strongly and I felt the tired cramp of a night's rowing. A persistent seabird called and I felt sleepy.

'Pylos? That is your name? Find Jason.'

Medea's words seemed to blend with a seabird call. I was sleepy and they did not make sense. I blinked as she spoke again, looking at her. They made sense then.

'Go on. He's making arrangements to hand over my dead body.' She held up one of the large sickle earrings I had seen among her black ringlets. The silver inside edge glinted, razor sharp. She rested it against her thigh. 'That is all he will have.'

A cut thigh-artery pumps out the blood in moments. No wonder Medea had gone ashore with such dignity. She was the only one who would decide her fate.

I rose. 'Lady, you are the bravest woman I have ever met.'

She smiled and shrugged, answering in a faraway voice that chilled me — as though she were speaking to someone unseen. 'The Mother knows what must be done.'

The sickle was pressed to her thigh. Her other hand idly trickled sand. So I turned and began walking across the island to the other side. Only some hundred yards; it was very small. On the ridge was a large lumpy stone with engraved spirals and deep-cut wide eyes. I circled around it, the eyes seeming to follow.

This little island brooded, close and hot. From the ridge I could see the Colchis galleys offshore. Apsyrtus had kept his promise and come alone. He and Jason would make their oaths over bread and salt and wine, sealing their agreement. And I was trudging through the hot sand to say it did not matter. By now Medea's blood would be making a dark crimson puddle in the sand. Jason had been too smart for himself.

Ahead was a small beach, fringed with brown tussock. A red-legged shorebird scuttled away and I heard her chicks cheeping in the nest. I was tired and my head ached. I stumbled down the last incline, pebbles sliding underfoot. The noise would warn them I was coming but that did not matter now.

I was right. It did not matter.

Jason and Apsyrtus were by two rocks, a smooth patch of sand between them. I saw Apsyrtus first. The Colchis prince lay on his stomach like a man asleep. Sand-midges hovered around his nose and flies buzzed also, attracted by the spreading patch of red blood under his arm. I knew that because the dagger was still there, dripping blood in the hand of the killer ...

Jason.

He stood on the other side, his eyes half-shut.

Breathing heavily as though he had been running. But there was no sweat upon his skin; he had not been running. He had been murdering.

The proof lay before me — the little spilled wine flask and two cups, the bread cakes and salt. They had sat down to eat and drink as was proper. But Apsyrtus's cup was overturned. Jason had made to fill it, the dagger, hidden up his wrist, flicked out the way he had once shown me. A killing thrust into the armpit — so quick that Apsyrtus was dead before his eyelids shut.

'You killed him,' I said.

I don't think Jason knew, till then, that I was there. Even though I was in full view of him. He turned very slowly and looked at the red blood on his blade. The dagger I had given him. I think the full horror came on us both then, like a ship smashing into rocks. The host killing his guest, worst of crimes — worst — nothing pardoned that. And I was witness to murder. Jason and I thought of that at the same time.

I took a step back. But I could not get away. Jason, warrior-prince, would have caught me within moments. He even thought of it, his leg-muscles tensing in the cross-strapped sandals, as though ready to spring. Then he let his dagger hand fall.

'Killing?' He mumbled the word as though very tired.

I was still poised to run. 'Killing ...?' a question still in my words — I did not want to believe this!

'Killing and oath-breaking.' His words still mumbled. 'Do you think that is the worst a man can do?' Clenching his bloodstained dagger. 'Yes, you would.'

He grinned, more an unpleasant stretch of his lips over his teeth. 'Pylos, the life of a peasant is simple. But kings and princes do not lead simple lives.'

He stopped. Meaning to say more, I think, but it all became too much. He flashed the dagger in his hand, suddenly throwing it high into the blue sky, splashing it into the blue-green water.

'There, I have destroyed your good gift!' he yelled. There was rage and puzzled madness in his voice. 'Kings and princes must do things that would turn your stomach!' The words burst out, his face like a black squall. 'They must do whatever they have to!'

Now he was sinking to his knees, his sand-encrusted hands over his eyes; big tears rolled over knuckles clenched so white I thought he would blind himself. Jason, who guided us all this way. Who pitted his wits against King Aeetes to keep us alive in Colchis. Who went so boldly into that snake-haunted temple. For himself, for his ambitions, also for us. He threw my dagger away, from shame — and because he did not trust his own hand. He might have killed me too.

I pulled Jason up. We could not stay here; the Rhea-Mother presence was too strong. He staggered like a man drunk, caught deep in woman things and drowning in his own cleverness.

He was clever. But Medea was cleverer. He would take the Fleece to Icolos, title to his kingdom. But she made other conditions. Kill Apsyrtus or she would die by her own hand. Jason cared for her too much for that — love, and because, like the Fleece, she was a trophy. He was so clever that he forgot one thing.

The further you push into the old lands, the more

you find the old worship. We Greeks had gone from the Mother to a whole God Family. Gaia, Rhea, Cybele, call her what you like; in the unknown lands she was still strong. Her influence caught him, like wreckwood in a whirlpool. Jason got what he wanted but paid for it. By having his honour and self-respect cut away.

So, Medea, the priestess of Rhea-Mother, had her revenge on Apsyrtus her enemy — and on Jason, her shrine breaker.

He staggered less now, past the ridge. And she came towards us, walking in that assured hip-swinging way of hers. Her silver sickles were back on her ears, flashing in her black hair. She was singing a little chant like the sound of snakes hissing.

'Send men for the body,' she said and passed on.

Jason straightened himself as we walked to the beach. There, we were within sight of *Argos*. He still stumbled as though drunk; he hummed a little tune that I knew. About a man who lost his sandal crossing a river. Before he knew he was a prince.

Before he knew what princes had to do.

Behind us, on the far beach, even the seagulls had stopped screaming.

Four of our crew brought back Apsyrtus's body and flung it on the foredeck. Medea came aboard with them and we cast off. She must have known, though, that the Colchis galleys would follow — for the body of their prince and to recover the gold.

'We are still in trouble,' muttered Butes as our oars backed and splashed. 'They will want all our blood for this.'

He was right. But Medea had thought of that. She knew one terrible way to delay pursuit; one further revenge for Rhea-Mother.

The sea wind took our sail but the lean black dog-shapes of the Colchis galleys followed. Of course Medea knew they would; that is why she had Apsyrtus's body taken on board.

His own body would delay them.

Now Medea squatted on the foredeck. With a long knife, she cut chunks from her brother's body and threw them overboard. She gutted and jointed him, any part that would float. It was like tossing a trail of meat to a dog. The Colchis galleys stopped to pick up pieces of their dead prince. That is how she slowed them down.

We rowed. It was good to wrench at the oars and not look back to the foredeck. Anceaus, our helmsman, had to face forward and see what Medea did. He bowed his head and swallowed, as though holding in his vomit. Jason went back and took over the steering oar. He stared ahead, not sparing himself the sight of what Medea did.

We did not look but saw the pieces floating by. And heard the final splash as she heaved what was left of her brother's body over the side. By then it was light enough to float. We lifted our oars to let it pass. We sweated and our oar blades dripped water; even the bravest did not look.

So, the Colchis galleys slowed to pick up the bobbing remains. A strong wind filled our sail and we drew away. We lost sight of them and I never want to see Colchis again. There were bloodstains on the foredeck now and Medea scooped water over them with a baler; whistling that high little tune as she did. When some of us turned, she was sitting back against the prow and staring over the blue sea.

Jason stood at the steering oar. His face blank, he heaved at the oar as though hoping his heart would burst. Still caught deep in his nightmare, knowing that he was so trapped.

I did not like Medea. I feared her. But, at the same time, I respected that she did not make excuses for what she had done. Her princely brother would have done something just as terrible to us, perhaps even broken his oath and killed us all. The hate between them was like that. But she was strong enough not to excuse herself. What she did was for Rhea-Mother and without shame.

And as the sail filled, Jason gave the steering oar back to Anceaus and walked down to the foredeck. Medea drew in her legs and let him sit down. Neither of them spoke.

So our voyage home began.

Chapter 20

We were on our way home but more death lay ahead.
Butes, the simple honest warrior who first helped
me, was killed. Hunting for wild honey on an island,
he fell down a gully and broke his neck. He had not
even time for a last joke before he died.

The dangers were not so frightening. Even the
Clashing Rocks were somehow set in place as
though the earth-shaking beneath them had
stopped. Mopsus screeched that they had not
stopped us from the unknown seas, so had lost their
power. I did not believe him but remembered how he
fought in Colchis square with the others. So we
pulled back through those narrow straits, without
needing a white dove to flutter ahead.

Phineus and his wife were gone too. The hawks
and kites still clustered thickly around their headland. I supposed that, like all frauds, he had made
one bad prophecy too many. And our voyage luck
held through the Hellespont. No Trojan galleys
barred our passage; they were away chasing pirates.
So we pulled into the good welcome waters of our
Greek sea.

Medea said almost nothing on the voyage. She
stayed on the stern. Each night when we put ashore,
she went off with Jason to sleep away from us. Most
of the time she looked over our heads, as though she
were still on her throne. She had power in her bearing, like a dark cloak. I wondered if she would lose

her power as we drew away from these lands where Rhea-Mother was so strong.

She did not. Other deaths would come from *Argos's* voyage; one many years later when I thought the shadow was passed.

As we neared Greek shorelines, we began losing men. Champions and heroes would not sail past their homes, but take their share of gold and go. News would spread quickly about the great fish-sea with coasts of iron and gold. Ten ships would go, then fifty, two hundred. Even though Troy barred the way; even then the kings of Greece had plans for Troy.

I rowed now, as one of the crew. Jason spoke as much or as little to me as he did to the others. He and Medea kept together a lot. But as our numbers fell off and *Argos* slowed, he rowed more. Two nights before Icolos landfall, we pulled up at the beach where Heracles had made such fun of our heroes.

I was nearly three years older now, near man-size, one of the crew, not the ship's boy who made the fires and served food. I would never be afraid of someone like Thegus again. I saw him once more, two years later in Athens harbour; we did not speak because he was hanging from a gallows, sun-dried as any filleted cod.

Jason walked a little way inland to a small village. They said Heracles was back and had done even more fantastic things. He had killed a giant boar and fought the three-headed dog who guards the entrance to Hades-underworld. The legends about Heracles grow and grow every year.

On the way back, Jason stopped within sight of the campfires. Medea was gone on some private business of woman-prayer. He said, 'Pylos, that gold arm ring Medea gave you. It will make you somebody in your village.'

'I won't go back,' I said. I was grown past that.

Jason went down to the campfire and returned with a plate of bread, meat and dried figs. The only time I was served my food by a prince. We ate together in silence a time. 'If I get my birthright in Icolos,' said Jason carefully, 'there will be a place for you.'

I had thought about that. And I think he knew my answer before I spoke. 'Lord Jason, I will stay on ships. I have seen the unknown world. Now I want to see the known world.'

'Because of what happened on the island.' He said it as a statement, not a question. Then he said something I did not expect. There is always a distance between noble and common folk. Only this once, on this stony beach, did it not matter. 'Pylos, you are the only one on this voyage who is not a noble or a prince. So tell me why it happened.'

I did not understand why he asked me that question. Years later I did. He knew all his reasons for such a terrible deed, but he was thinking about the road to that island, limping on one sandal. So I did not think about the island, or that road from the mountains. I swallowed a mouthful of bread and thought hard.

'Lord Jason, heroes and princes are not ordinary people. I thought they were always better in everything they did.' I stopped, still thinking hard. 'I expected more of them than was real.'

'Go on.' Jason groaned the words in the darkness.

'You are a prince. But you came from a mountain village. You thought it was enough to act like them. You expected more than was real and that led you on.'

'Princes do what they must,' replied Jason, looking into the darkness.

Yes, he thought that. Because when this voyage began, he thought like me. In simple clear terms of nobles, heroes and commoners. And, over all this time, realising where it led — to the sudden killing thrust, to blood and seagulls screaming on that beach.

We sat together, looking over to where *Argos* lay moored; the special gleaming moonlight of our own dark sea. Yes, I wanted to stay with Jason, the prince who voyaged to legend. But I was remembering the blood on his iron knife — kings and princes do not lead simple lives!

Now I sensed the presence of Medea, somewhere close and listening. That made me uneasy, so I rose. 'Lord, I will always thank you.'

Jason rose too, his old grin loosening; still darkness in his eyes. 'You have nothing to thank me for, Pylos. I wish you good voyaging.'

'Thank you, Lord.'

So we made landfall in Icolos harbour. A great crowd cheered us ashore and gaped at the gold. King Pelias stayed in his palace, and there went Jason and Medea with the Fleece. Pelias gave them a great banquet; from his high windows, he would have heard the crowd shouting for Jason.

Our great company of heroes split up quickly. Castor and Pollux to Sparta, Calais and Zetes stayed with Jason. Other heroes went to their homelands. Orpheus played a sad lilt of passing before he went. Anceaus was taking passage; good to see his big cheerful nod when I asked if I could go with him.

So we sailed on the morning tide, the palace and town still dark, passing *Argos*, empty; her mast unstepped, her figurehead shining blank as though robbed of a living spirit. I had not seen Jason again. And would not see him for many years. Only when the last death happened.

Rhea-Mother never forgets.

I stayed some years with Anceaus. He taught me to be a steersman. In time I became a shipmaster of war galleys in the service of Tiryns. We raided far as the shores of Egypt but I grew tired of fire and death. I mastered merchant ships after that.

In bits and pieces, from gossip and the songs of bards, I heard about the *Argos* crew.

I think it was Calais and Zetes who killed Hylas; they were telling the others when I found them. They never forgave Heracles for humbling them. He tracked them down and killed them. Sons of the North Wind? Heracles balanced a rock over their graves so it would sway in every breeze.

Castor and Pollux fell out with two other great warriors, Lynceaus and Idas — a fight over women. Idas boasted a little too much, too often. After the fight, only Pollux was alive. Victory could not console him for the life of his twin; he killed himself.

I heard of the others too. Up and down the shores of the known world, to adventure, kingship or death. Telamon became king, father of the great

Ajax. Some just died, some were not heard of again. Of course, though, I heard about Jason.

He did not get the throne of Icolos. King Pelias died suddenly (people often did, around Medea) but the fickle mob made someone else king. Jason went to Corinth. He dared too much and courted a Corinth princess. Medea's answer was devastating; she killed their children and left him.

Nobody knows where she went. Back to Colchis perhaps, to take her chance with the new power structure. She took the Fleece with her. Even now I cannot call her evil. She had her duty as a daughter of Rhea-Mother. She was strong, powerful and dangerous. Jason should have left her on the island. He took one chance too many.

Years later, just before the Troy Expedition, I went to Corinth. I was a shipmaster, part of the *Argos* legend, commanding boys as young as I had been. I did not marry because I was wary of women. Nor did I return to Lemnos; once I saw a group of their priest-women ashore at Athens, to worship at the Athena shrine there. One was just like Ixlos, young enough to be her daughter. I watched her out of sight but never dared ask.

So I was shipmaster, rough with the ship boys but only to toughen them. They seemed to respect me. Always I had a hollow place inside. I had never really thanked Jason and I should have; the more I lived of life, the more I knew this. Then King Idomenus of Crete hired me to command the sailing of his black-hulled war galleys to Troy. It will be good to see that proud city burn.

On the way, he visited Corinth. One king meeting another.

Bad days were around us like the first hint of a storm. The coast shook and rumbled as though earth-shaking Poseidon were angry about our plans for his city. The unknown sea trade only trickled because the horse tribes were fighting each other, but Greeks were on those shores, building in stone. Tense bad days, as we waited for the Troy storm to break.

I had heard Jason stayed at the palace. So I kept to the harbour, not wishing to meet him. But Rhea-Mother decided otherwise. I went for a walk down the beach and saw something that turned twenty years into yesterday. The full flood of good and bad memory.

Jason brought the *Argos* to Corinth. When the ship grew rotten with age, as all ships do, it was dragged ashore; propped up against the sea wall. There, before me now, was the great ship that had taken us so far — without a mast, rowing benches and steering oars gone for firewood, her ribbed belly, stern and foredeck black with age. The arched prow, stripped of gilt, still towered over.

And from its shadow, a thin voice called.

An old man's voice. I went closer and looked at him. His white hair straggled over sunken cheeks; his nose was red-veined from too much wine. His thin shoulders were wrapped in a cloak. His red-rimmed eyes as sharp as ever, ran over me.

'You made a man of yourself, Pylos.'

'I learned about life,' I replied.

It was a very cold and gusty day. Above Jason, the

old prow shook, its shadow flickering like a warning finger. He grinned, that famous grin, now showing broken yellow teeth. He put out a thin hand. Not like a prince offering reassurance; like an old man needing understanding.

I took his hand. His fingers had no more strength than seaweed and they shook. There were things I wanted to say to him, full on my tongue and closed lips. I could not though. He saw that in my face and took his hand away.

'Storms and earthquakes these days.' He huddled in his cloak and grinned up. 'You still don't understand what princes have to do.'

The prow still shook, its black shadow-finger waggled. 'I know you should not sit here,' I replied.

'There is much I should not have done, Pylos. Good voyaging ...' he broke off. I think he nearly called me 'boy' again.

So he dismissed me. Too proud to see the pity in my face. I walked on down the beach, stunned as a man thrown on rocks. Inside myself I was running. After twenty years voyaging I was my own man; there is nobody more independent than a shipmaster. But on this cold storm-driven beach, with black clouds over the high limestone walls of Corinth, I felt like a boy again.

I was back on that island, Jason's hands over his face, tears running through his sandy fingers; on the stony beach, asking me about himself because he truly did not know. I had worshipped Jason and hated him. He destroyed his honour and self-respect to save us all. So, all these years gone, I could not walk away.

The wind blew harder as I turned. The fishermen were pulling up their boats. The first lightning forked itself down like yellow cracks in the black sky. It outlined the high prow of *Argos* and the cloak-wrapped figure who sat underneath.

Lightning comes from All-Father Zeus. But even fathers are born of women and, cold as the rain, I felt Rhea-Mother touch me. So I turned to run back but my feet caught in something, thick as mud and clear as springwater. The pebbly beach wavered, another bright blast of lightning spitted down; also came the first strong punch of an icy stormwind.

Ahead, etched in sudden black shadows, the prow of *Argos* shook. The painted yellow eyes were chipped and faded, as though blind. Then the prow fell, fast and hard as the innocence of my youth. A thunderclap followed, shaking the clouds like a storm-cloak. Then silence.

The fishermen were clustered, scared. I pushed between them and knelt. Jason lay there, his face buried in the sand; I scooped it from his nose to let him breathe. My own hand shook like rigging taut in wind. His hand, knuckles swollen with age-joint pains, clutched the pale sand tightly. More blasting thunder and snapping yellow lightning; the heavy rotten timbers shivered but could do no more harm. The prow was crushed between Jason's shoulders; his clutching hand was rigid and stiff.

'Jason, Lord!' I grabbed his rigid hand in both of mine and leaned over, whispering and shouting at the same time. 'I did learn about life from you — to go on! Thank you, Lord.'

No answer came. His hand closed in mine. My

tears felt icy as the storm wind coming. I held onto his hand so long that one of my crew pulled us apart. And they prised off the black rotten wood, gently pulled his body clear. Gently, because I screamed at them to do so; he was Jason, prince and voyager ...

They used the timbers of *Argos* as his funeral pyre. I sat on my foredeck and watched the black smoke go up into the sky. The storm still blew, shredding it against the grey clouds; the yellow lightning crackled like a hag's laughter. Later I would pour wine on the ashes and say prayers. That Jason would still be a prince in Hades-underworld. The black smoke tattering into strips and nothing. His legend though, would never die.

I am glad I ran back. I don't know if he heard me say those words. But I am glad that I did. Said earlier, they might have moved him from his death place. Can you avoid the vengeance of the Mother? I will always think his fingers tightened that final time into mine.

I have to believe that they did. Just as Jason believed in himself.

You have to believe in something.

The Curse
of the Darkling Mill

Otfried Preussler

Drawn by powers beyond his control, fourteen-year-old Krabat finds himself apprenticed to a mill in the fens. There the homeless orphan begins work with the Miller's eleven other journeymen.

But strange things happen at the mill. Time passes at an unnatural pace, and the journeymen have super-human powers, and can turn themselves into ravens and other creatures. Trapped by an evil power which makes escape impossible, Krabat is forced to submit to the Master of the mill.

He begins to learn the Secret Arts, but discovers that every New Year's Eve one of the miller's men must die ...

The Curse of the Darkling Mill is an eerie tale of sorcery and nightmares, which will keep you guessing right to the end.

"As soon as I saw the title ... I knew I would love it! ... it grabbed my attention immediately."
Education Otherwise

Flyways

A Flute in Mayferry Street

Eileen Dunlop

A long-forgotten letter, a faded photograph and a crumpled jacket – the Ramsays' normally quiet life is about to be thrown into disarray as their old town house comes alive with the whispering and haunting melody of a flute.

Colin and his disabled sister, Marion, search for answers to these clues from the past, never realizing where they may lead.

What they discover reveals a family secret hidden by historic events, and with repercussions for their own lives.

A Flute in Mayferry Street is an inspiring tale of the magic of dreams and the power of the supernatural.

Flyways

Five Days of the Ghost

William Bell

Exploring a sacred Indian burial ground in the middle of the night isn't Karen's idea of a great start to the holidays. But she lets her brother, John, talk her into it and that night they row across the lake to the forbidden island.

What they find there plunges them into a world they never thought existed; a world where past and present blend and the spirits of the dead communicate with the living.

With the help of John's schoolfriend, Weird Noah, an expert on the supernatural, Karen and John try to unravel the mystery which suddenly invades their lives and fills their home with strange happenings.

Fascinated and afraid. Karen is forced to confront the tragic events in her life that she has refused to face up to now.

> " ... the best book I have ever read."
> Emma Irwin

Flyways